T0307395

# Forty Acres

by
Gerard Murrin

Robert D. Reed Publishers • Bandon, OR

Robert D. Reed Publishers
P.O. Box 1992
Bandon, OR 97411
Phone: 541-347-9882 • Fax: -9883
E-mail: 4bobreed@msn.com
web site: www.rdrpublishers.com

**Typesetting by Barbara Kruger**
**Cover Design by Grant Prescott**
**Cover Photograph by Liz Cockrum, ©2006**
**<http://www.lizcockrum.com>www.lizcockrum.com**

ISBN 978-1-931741-74-3

Library of Congress Control Number 2006900420

Manufactured, typeset and printed in the United States of America

# Chapter 1

He'd been waiting patiently for her to come out of the store. But unexpectedly the woman emerged from the backseat of the limousine that'd been lingering out front. The door remained open long enough for Sanders to identify the other passenger. "Holy ----," he gasped, slinking deeper into the seat of his rented vehicle. The man he caught a glimpse of was quite possibly the most recognized developer in the state. What was she doing with him? Wasn't he the enemy? Tom hadn't anticipated learning much from where he'd parked but now he couldn't believe what he was witnessing.

Just last night he'd expressed his disappointment. "I feel like I'm being punished," he said, "banished to a distant outpost." Actually, though, Tom was the one who advised against all of them attending the auction and that's how he ended up being relegated the remote observation post in the first place. "It'd be way too risky for the whole lot of us being seen together looking chummy," Tom cautioned. His fellow council members agreed and, considering he was their president, they urged him to keep a low profile. Since he wouldn't be inside he pleaded for the others to provide "a vivid account" of everything they saw. "Take note of who's interested in which properties."

His passion and knowledge for the issues earned Sanders nomination for the society's presidency in only his third year of membership. Other members had grown to trust Tom and quickly placed confidence in his leadership abilities. This was rather remarkable considering the highly secretive nature of the society and the length of time normally required before one was accepted into their inner circle.

Before he left for his post that morning, Tom contacted each member of the voting council to review individual assignments. Andy Cemanski wasn't pleased when he received the first call.

"For Christ's sake, Tom. What was the meeting for last night? Haven't we been through all of this already?"

"Of course we have, Andrew," Tom reassured him. "However, you know as well as I that properties of this size haven't gone to bid for some time now. God knows there aren't very many like these left. So let's be darn sure that we do our best with this opportunity."

"Opportunity?" Andy mumbled as he clicked off his direct link device. "We're just buying time. Before long there won't be anything left."

Andy stood a shade under six feet four inches tall and carried a swagger that belied a man who'd reached the latter half of his sixties living life hard all along the way. In his younger days, Andy provided the muscle for their cause. Those were more violent times when there seemed to be so much more to be won or lost. But Andy was more than just muscle. His courage and cunning inspired others and, after gaining a bit of wisdom, he rose to become the society's first true leader. Andy was still held in high enough esteem to retain his seat on the voting council, but he had relinquished his ultimate leadership position years ago. After giving several others a try, Tom Sanders became their new leader and he took a more careful, calculating approach than Andy ever had.

"Hell, in my day, we didn't take any crap from the developers," Andy told Tom the previous evening. "When word got out that they were about to strip topsoil, six or seven of us would get up early and go camp out on the property. The foreman would always drive up first. He'd see us sitting there and just turn around and leave. For some reason he'd never want to talk to us on his own," Cemanski said while a sly grin crept across his face. "Then, an hour or so later, he'd come back with his boss and a few goons and that's when the fun would start."

Despite intermittent bouts of irritation over Tom's fascination with details and what seemed to be his never-ending preparation, Andy had learned to admire Tom. He sensed that the playing field had changed and that the society needed a new approach. Just maybe, a man like Tom Sanders could keep the flame alive. Nevertheless, Andy had been fighting too long to completely change his ways and his chest of dreams was almost empty.

Truth be told, it had been Andy's approach that necessitated a change in their practices and had forced the society underground. Even though he looked fondly upon the old days, Andy knew past actions hamstrung what measures the group could take today. The flamboyant raids he led had made them a nuisance in the eyes of some and finally resulted in the government officially banning their society. So Tom was right. They had to be careful and methodically take what gains they could.

Andy's assignment that morning was to walk into the county building, sit down, and blatantly observe everything that transpired. Ironically, his notoriety is what made him the least obtrusive for this role. Presiding magistrates would undoubtedly take notice of Andy because, after all, he was still the fabled leader of the LPS. But he'd receive little scrutiny because he'd been scrutinized so many times before. Auction officials would see him and idly say, "There's the gruff old man unable to let go of a lost cause."

# Chapter 2

The concept of holding an auction to sell reclaimed land seemed antiquated. The world bear witness to great inventions and various revolutionary ages: industrial, transportation, technology, communication and beyond. But for every new idea intended to make life easier there always seemed to be a crackpot scheming to outwit the inventor and make life more complicated. The result being that hardly a sole trusted whatever latest technology the government came up with to re-dispense their ever-dwindling commodity. The public wanted to see exactly how land was being sold and who was buying it. So Ogle County, like many municipalities across the country, found that the simple public auction minimized suspicion and had decided to revert to this ancient medium as a means to distribute land several years back. Therefore, it seemed appropriate that the LPS should employ the ancient art of spying; using human eye and ear to find out what was really going on behind the scenes of these supposedly open proceedings.

Tom Sanders had suggested that Jason McAlpin stake out at the Greenery Restaurant, a favorite breakfast gathering for local politicians and businesspeople. The Greenery was across the street, halfway down the block from the county building and the irony of the restaurant's name in an expanding desert of pavement was not lost on McAlpin. McAlpin sipped on a bottomless cup of coffee attempting to look preoccupied with his hand-held computer and modular communication device. Jason's real mission was to carefully monitor everyone who came in and out of the restaurant that morning. "Most bidding agents are convinced their direct link communiqués are intercepted so they'll use the Greenery as a rendezvous on their way to auction. There they'll receive last minute instructions from their bosses and unscrupulous bureaucrats alike," Sanders had told Jason.

While her dad fidgeted in his booth, McAlpin's daughter held position at the Rexford Hotel directly across from the county building. The Rexford was a probable stopover for the out-of-town developers interested in today's auction. Conveniently, the previous week, the young lady had been hired as a night clerk and as an aspiring LPS member she gladly accepted her father's instructions to conduct surveillance from the hotel's lobby until her shift ended at 10 a.m. She studied every face that appeared and strained to hear every whisper trying to be nonchalant while her imagination ran rampant.

Sanders assumed a less conspicuous position near the county building's parking garage. He mounted a small video monitor on the dashboard and aimed the lens directly at the garage entrance to record the tags of every tiny, electric vehicle that entered or exited.

Robert Sonnvoldt and Tamara Hopkins took the lead roles and would be at the auction actively participating in the bidding process. Sonnvoldt, descendent of one of the earliest farming families in Ogle County, would attempt to lay claim to a certain property in the northwest corner. Auction officials were unlikely to allow for a "farmstead exception" but it was worth making a try. However, if that didn't work he'd argue that lineal title to the property had been improperly broken and attempt to win the bid under an "ancestral claim."

Most government officials had no sympathy for "farmsteaders". In today's age, they contributed nothing to the community as far as the politicians were concerned. "Farmers don't fill the coffers," the saying went. No matter how any of them tried to twist the law there wasn't a politician who'd ever figured out how to extract more tax from a farmer than from the "fools" the developers reeled in for them. However, occasionally the government would save a farmstead here or there. They felt it placated those making an argument for keeping a small local crop in the event of a national catastrophe. "Nonsense," the more hardened officials responded. "The 'Agricultural' counties provide more than is needed and if there ever was a disaster imagine the anarchy that would ensue if we tried to allocate our local crop. It'd be better that we had no crop at all."

So in all likelihood the ever-weakening farmstead argument wouldn't win Robert the prize. He stood a better chance raising doubt via the ancestral claim. Auction administrators might be inclined to proceed cautiously and hear out such a claim because there were still enough independent-minded citizens who didn't like the idea of the government running rough shod over family property rights.

Meanwhile, as Robert was trying to make his lineal-tainted farmstead purchase, Tamara Hopkins would be attempting to make a purchase under quite a different pretense. Tamara would pose as a small business owner trying to break into a development industry dominated by sometimes ruthless, sometimes collegial power brokers. Her presence would be in sharp contrast to what auction officials were accustomed to seeing. They would be taken by her beauty, no doubt, but they'd also be asking, "where's her team of lawyers and how's a novice going to compete with the large, well-schooled developers?" Tom Sanders was banking on this contrast working to their favor. "How bold would it be to send one of our own in to bid on a property posing as a developer?" Tom had asked rhetorically. Even Andy Cemanski liked this part of the plan. It wasn't the literal "knock 'em in the chops" method that he had preferred utilizing in the "old" days but, metaphorically speaking, it was awful darn close.

She needed to be alluring in order to garner attention yet modest enough to generate sympathy. This was the angle she'd attempt to exploit because although the larger developers almost always seemed to prevail they were subject to a certain amount of grumbling from the citizenry and lower level bureaucrats. "The process is rigged," some would say. "Agreements are made ahead of time. Parcels are doled out so that they each keep a share of the pie." The more reform minded officials were sensitive to these comments. They didn't want the public to think that they were merely the developers' pawns. These were the officials who wanted the auction process to at least look as if it were fair. Occasionally the reformers pushed for someone else to become part of the mix; someone outside the big three locals and handful of regional developers who normally won all the bids. Perhaps Tamara could be that someone.

Most of the auction attendees would know nothing about the newcomer; however, there were certain interested parties who would do their homework. As was customary for those who planned to make a serious bid, Tamara pre-registered for the auction. This subjected her to the inevitable background screening by auction officials who, in turn, passed all the information they gathered along to the major developers to avoid their wrath for failing to keep them informed.

One of the developers who received information from the government was John Gardner. Of course, Gardner didn't trust the thoroughness of the government's research so he often had his staff prepare their own report. The dossier in front of him read, "Tamara Hopkins graduated summa cum laude from Northwestern University. She immediately enrolled in law school at the same institution and studied for two more years before leaving to study abroad. She returned three years later; however, there's no verification that she ever received her law degree. She worked at a major bank for several years before starting her own business consulting practice. The business has been quite successful but has not been involved in development, property management, construction or any project related to real estate." In fact, the report provided to John Gardner didn't indicate that Ms. Hopkins even owned any real estate. "She's unmarried and rents a fairly luxurious two-bedroom town home approximately ten miles east of Ogletown," the report stated.

This must be the key, Gardner thought as he continued to peruse the dossier. "Hopkins' parents had owned a reasonably large development company in Kane County. They retired over ten years ago and now live in Texas. Interestingly, they just closed shop. They never made an attempt to sell the business despite its apparent value, particularly seeing as their retirement coincided with the peak of the last major consolidation in the development industry."

Gardner grinned and said aloud to himself, "So little Tammy wants to resurrect what her parents left behind."

# Chapter 3

The gavel banged promptly at 9:00 a.m. and the auction was underway. Nearly five hundred people filled the auction hall of the modern county building that day. The building had been constructed a decade before in the heart of Ogletown to replace the old, crumbling courthouse. The hall's audience sat in rows of low-backed chairs that were separated by wide aisles and rose gradually to form a crescent around a central podium flanked by tables reserved for presiding officials. Only serious bidders were expected to take a seat in the first three rows and as a result the participants gathered there were often referred to as Ogle County's Real Estate Hall of Fame. "More like Hall of Shame," Andy Cemanski preferred to make reference.

Robert Sonnvoldt entered the hall first. Sonnvoldt was considered a good looking man by most, sandy-haired and six feet tall, but he was of the type that blended into his surroundings and today the denim pants and long-sleeved working shirt that he wore made him look as much the relic of the county's bygone farming era as he had intended. Tamara Hopkins, on the other hand, looked stunning in her neat-fitting business attire. The tawny colored jacket with matching skirt and heels accentuated her flowing chestnut brown hair. She pulled this hair away from her cheeks, behind her ears to permit anyone who choose notice— and there were many who did—view to a most charming visage. As Robert and Tamara settled into their seats on opposite ends of the seventh row, a forty-acre parcel on the eastern side of the county was presented for bid. It was the smallest parcel on the docket that morning and was situated in an already heavily developed area. The parcel was a "fill-in" and not worth a tremendous commotion but the right developer could generate a decent profit from the investment. Neither one of the contrasting undercover LPS agents was planning to show much interest in the property. Although the society was concerned with various configurations of open space, this property was of a size and in an area that was hardly worth the fight. The society had finite resources and needed to pick its spots wisely.

Gardner Development Company, or GDC as they were commonly known, opened the bid. Tamara made the next bid not intending for it to be the winning bid but hoping that an early offer would establish her presence at the auction. "One hundred thousand per," she declared in a loud, clear voice attempting to project confidence.

If attracting attention was Tamara's only aim, then the reaction she received showered her with unimaginable success. Everyone took notice. After her bid the entire gallery turned to stare at the newcomer. Who was this stunning, impeccably dressed woman? Tamara stared back feeling their eyes as if they were lasers boring through her soul. The crowd's silence would not end; there were no counters to follow her offer. What have I done, she fret. What kind of stupid risk did I take? Isn't anyone else going to bid? I've used up four million of our resources for land, which may well already be lost.

Stunned, she could faintly hear the auctioneer say, "Going once" before another voice boomed, "One hundred and five!"

The bid came from a representative of Manetti Homes, the fifth largest but, more realistically, the smallest developer remaining in Ogle County. From there, the action picked up and Tamara managed a deep breath. Newton Residential was also interested in the property and the two homebuilders countered back and forth. The property eventually went to Manetti Homes for one hundred and fifty thousand dollars per acre. Tamara was thankful that the bidding finally resumed after her call but, at the same time, she realized that the hefty price the small parcel garnered was a harbinger for what the society would need to spend today if it had any hope of acquiring a property.

The second subject presented was an eighty-acre parcel located in the central part of the county on Prairie Parkway less than ten miles from where they were gathered. The property was immediately adjacent to a very large tract owned by GDC. The GDC land was still vacant and the company's plans for the property, although filed with the Office of Land Management, had not been made public. Normally, intentions for a project were made public immediately. However, the OLM had the discretion to withhold development plans for up to one year if the developer could demonstrate good cause. In this case, John Gardner had personally requested that construction plans be kept under wrap so that was cause enough as far as the OLM was concerned.

On the other side of the property currently up for bid, to the west, was another vacant parcel. This particular parcel was two hundred and forty acres and just happened to be the third property that would go to bid today. The third subject was a beautiful piece of land but way too expensive for the society's budget. They would need more than a little luck just to obtain the eighty-acre parcel.

The second bid began at one hundred and twenty thousand. The society's council members were sure that this parcel would go for more than the first but by how much they could nary a guess. There were too many factors involved to predict the range in pricing where a property might fall. The previous night, the council had reached a compromise and gave Tamara a budget of one hundred and seventy-five thousand dollars per acre. Andy disagreed with Tom's insistence on establishing a budget cap. "Come on, Tom," he implored. "Don't tie her hands. If we're intending to make a splash, then let's make a splash!"

Robert Sonnvoldt joined Andy's side. "We have to be more aggressive. Otherwise, every square inch of land in this county will be gone before we know it."

They argued the matter for several minutes before Tamara turned the tide in Tom's favor. "I believe Tom is right," she stated. "We shouldn't bid any higher than one seventy, maybe one seventy-five. Remember, gentlemen, acquiring property was not our primary objective when we first planned attending this auction. We wanted to use this auction as a means to understanding what tricks the developers are playing and for finding out who's padding the County Clerk's pockets. We don't need to deplete our resources by acquiring land that we're not sure what we're going to do with anyway."

Andy stopped squabbling after Tamara made her point. He realized that Tom was much more in tune with what was happening in the county than he was. Tom was a good man and he should trust his judgment. However, it was probably Tamara's comment that the society "wasn't sure what they were going to do with the eighty-acre parcel" that took the most wind out of Andy's argument. The big war for land in this county has been lost, Andy lamented. Now we're fighting for scraps that we wouldn't know what do with even if we had them.

Robert Sonnvoldt stopped arguing once Tamara made her point as well. When he looked into Tamara's mesmerizing green eyes he melted. He could join Andy to challenge Tom, but he wouldn't dare take sides against both Tom and Tamara. Such were the forces of group dynamics and, more so, such was the force of Robert's infatuation for Tamara. So the following morning there was Tamara, in the county building, hoping to win the bid on parcel number two but recognizing her limitations given the one seventy-five per acre budget she had helped impose. Up until that moment she'd considered fourteen million dollars to be an enormous sum of money.

Unlikely as it might later be proved Tamara tried reasoning that the winning bid on the first parcel would establish the going rate at one hundred and fifty thousand per acre. Bidding on the second parcel was proceeding methodically towards that target and Cranstead Commercial appeared to be the only other interested bidder. Maybe they would stop at one fifty.

"Does anyone have one-five-five?" the auctioneer called.

"Yes," Tamara nodded and then glanced furtively toward Cranstead's representative. She saw no indication and the longer he sat motionless the more excited she became. Had she actually won the bid? But a few moments later, a woman from across the aisle calmly called, "One sixty."

As Tamara registered who had made the bid her eyes cast downward and she quietly exhaled. It was a representative of GDC tendering their first offer. She realized that if GDC were choosing to enter the bidding at this point it was likely that they were willing to blow right past her budget allowance. The question that they'd be able to outbid her was not in doubt. Tamara was contemplating the sense of even trying to counter when suddenly she heard Cranstead increase their offer.

Upon hearing the Cranstead counter, John Gardner leaned forward in his chair to catch the attention of his bidding agent. The woman immediately sensed Gardner's shift and looked over to see him nod. She clearly understood her boss's intent; outbid Cranstead Commercial.

As Chairman of Gardner Development Company, the largest developer in Ogle County, John Gardner wielded a significant amount of power. He personally detested of Cranstead Commercial and occasionally had visions of crushing them. "Cranstead's projects are hideous," he privately told friend and enemy alike. Yet publicly, Gardner feigned tolerance for Cranstead. As one of the bigger players perhaps, he considered, it might be best that they stuck around. Gardner didn't want the government harboring any ideas that GDC was becoming a monopoly.

Gardner's public tolerance for his competitor could only go so far; however., Cranstead was not going to outbid him for any property that he really wanted and parcel number two, like the third property that would go to bid, was on Prairie Parkway. "Don't let that guy shoehorn between my properties," Gardner instructed his agent before the auction. Since GDC already owned the land east of parcel two, Gardner's statement implied that the larger parcel on the other side would also be his by day's end.

Bidding for parcel number two continued to one eighty-five before it appeared Cranstead was ready to concede. But surprises were to come and John Gardner sat stunned when he heard Tamara Hopkins proclaim, "One ninety."

Gardner glanced at the Cranstead agent after Tamara's bid. The man did indeed appear to have reached his limit. Tamara's offer was too high for Cranstead. Did the Hopkins woman know what she was doing, Gardner wondered? He contemplated for a while before thinking, what the heck, why not let her win the bid? She won't know what to do with the property anyway and then, once she figures out that she's land-locked between two GDC properties she'll decide to sell the eighty acres back to me. So John Gardner nonchalantly motioned to his bidding representative with a flat palm to indicate that they were done bidding. And like that, Tamara Hopkins had acquired the first piece of real estate she had ever owned in her life.

When the auctioneer declared "Sold," Tamara strode to the podium at the front of the room to sign a bid slip. As she made her way through the aisle back to her seat she caught Andy Cemanski's eye. "Land grabber," he said snidely in a voice loud enough to be heard by those around. Inside, however, Andy was beaming. Tamara had disregarded her budget and pushed forward to win the bid. He was proud of her. It was just the type of impulsive, aggressive behavior that he remembered employing in the good old days.

A murmur continued for a few moments as the assembly let the shock of what had just happened settle in. A newcomer had come in and stole the bid. In short order, however, the auctioneer banged the gavel again to start the process on parcel number three. Tamara wasn't about to bother placing a bid on this property. There was no way the society could afford it, especially after the fifteen million plus that she had just spent on the eighty-acre tract.

As the bidding resumed, many in attendance took notice when a tall, distinguished looking man somewhere in his mid-forties entered the room. Andy Cemanski recognized the man instantly and he sneered. Here was Arthur Flemming the head of Pinnacle Development, arguably the largest developer in the state. Apparently, the bidding on parcel number three was of concern to Mr. Flemming.

GDC came out strong to open the bid. Cranstead Commercial displayed token interest in the property, but Cemanski already sensed that they wouldn't be able to match GDC's earnest efforts to obtain this parcel.

Ballinger Builders, the second largest developer in the county, was showing no interest in the property at all. Cemanski suspected that GDC had struck a deal with Ballinger before the auction started. GDC wanted this land.

Just as GDC seemed set to win the bid Pinnacle Development's representative submitted their first offer. The assembly was humming again while John Gardner seethed. He had been astonished when he saw Arthur Flemming enter the hall and now, after hearing Pinnacle's bid, he searched his memory trying to come up with a connection on why Flemming's company would have an interest in acquiring a property on Prairie Parkway. Pinnacle had developments all over the state but had never bothered much with Ogle County. They were huge in DeKalb and Kane Counties to the east; however, Gardner could only think of one property that they had developed in his county. Perhaps Pinnacle was only testing the waters but, God knows, they have the resources to make a lot of noise here, Gardner bemoaned.

After Pinnacle's first offer the bidding continued back and forth. GDC would raise five thousand and then Pinnacle would counter with the same. Gardner grew tense but he dared not look to where Arthur Flemming was sitting. Finally, Gardner directed his bidding agent to stop for he had decided on a new strategy. He knew he could get parcel number two on Prairie Parkway back from the Hopkins woman if he wanted it, but since he didn't currently have it why be too aggressive on parcel number three? Gardner decided to conserve his resources for parcel number five, which he suddenly became convinced was the real prize of today's auction.

The gavel struck the podium indicating that Pinnacle Development had won parcel number three and the crowd buzzed. The audience was amazed at the heights the bids had reached on the first three properties. There were also whispers about Pinnacle Development. Most people knew who Pinnacle was, but no one was accustomed to seeing the company participate in the Ogle County auctions. And what made Arthur Flemming himself, chairman of the state's leading development firm, decide to attend the auction?

John Gardner certainly hadn't anticipated the course of events that transpired on the last two bids and his impatience didn't allow him to sit any longer. So, he quickly exited for the lobby before bidding on parcel number four commenced. He wanted to collect himself before the final bid of the day on parcel number five. Gardner's anxiety turned out to be fortuitous for the society.

Parcel number four was tucked away in the northwest corner beyond the Rock River, which was the one side of the county that as yet had retained some rural flavor. County government expected the northwest sector to be developed; however, most of the builders didn't have their infrastructure ready to make a serious move into the area. GDC was the only developer with sufficient depth and with a supply base, which would allow them to begin immediate expansion in the northwest. Therefore, the society expected that GDC would be their only competitor for the one hundred and twenty acre parcel.

GDC had discussed acquiring parcel number four in their auction-planning meeting, but they had made no definite plans. "Let's play this one by ear," Gardner told his team. "We'll see what happens with the first three bids and then see who decides to bid on number four. Then, we'll know how aggressive we'll need to be."

These ambiguous instructions instantly became a problem for GDC's bidding agent when John Gardner left the hall and left himself unavailable to provide her the necessary cues. When Robert Sonnvoldt opened the bidding on parcel number four she didn't know what to do. She had never seen Sonnvoldt at the auction before and had no idea who he was.

It seemed many people had decided to take a break after the excitement of the first three bids and the room was quiet when Sonnvoldt made his offer. However, Sonnvoldt's anonymity did draw the attention of Ballinger Builder's representative. "Point of order," the man called. "Who is this man and has he submitted a proper plan?" Although the extent of detail varied, all bidders were required to submit an application on or before the morning of the auction containing a development plan and a statement of their financial wherewithal. Larger developers had demanded such a procedure to deter inflated bids from amateurs who had neither government acceptable development plans nor the funds necessary to complete a project. The government appreciated this procedure as well because it averted time wasted chasing down information on illegitimate bidders after the fact.

An auction official stood up and looked toward Sonnvoldt. "So state your name."

"Robert Sonnvoldt."

The official then glanced at the desktop below him. He saw Sonnvoldt's name on the screen and said, "This man has filed an ancestral claim and he seeks a farmstead exception."

Some of the crowd groaned. A few others, including Andy Cemanski stood and clapped.

"If this man has an ancestral claim, why does he not already own the property?" the Ballinger representative demanded to know.

"It is a section 515 claim, sir," the official responded. "It's disputed. The government respects his claim but cannot unconditionally support it. Therefore, he must bid for the property."

"Does he have the financial wherewithal?" Ballinger's representative pressed.

"Inappropriate question, sir," the official responded. Auction officials had access to financial information from the application; however, it was held confidential, or at least supposed to be, in order to assure the integrity of the bidding process. It was only to be used at an auction official's discretion when necessary to put a halt to unsanctioned bidding.

After the exchange of order the room grew quiet again. The GDC bidder thought about raising Sonnvoldt's bid just to test his mettle. However, she didn't know what Gardner had intended so she remained silent. Sonnvoldt was awarded the property at his opening bid of seventy-five thousand per acre.

The final bid that day was anticlimactic after the surprises that took place earlier. GDC won the bid for a property located in the still relatively unpopulated southwest area. The land was a large stretch commonly known, but really only by people in that region, as Meador Farms. Meanwhile, Sonnvoldt, Hopkins and Cemanski all left the county building separately as the auction proceedings concluded and at the time no one in attendance seemed to come away with the impression that the three had any connection to each other. Yet all three left sharing in the same sensation of satisfaction and amazement. They couldn't believe that the society had just completed the acquisition of two properties. They had just saved two hundred acres of land.

# Chapter 4

"They'll be here soon," Tom Sanders said somewhat dejectedly as he looked into his wife's beautiful dark eyes, which accentuated the bronze skin that conveyed her Mexican heritage.

"I know. You should know better than to schedule a meeting for a Saturday evening," she pouted only partially in jest.

The council had agreed to wait several days before meeting. "Let's allow things to settle down a bit first," Sanders had advised. As it turned out Saturday was the day they picked to reconvene. Andy Cemanski arrived at the Sanders' residence first driving a car he borrowed from his son-in-law who had rented it for a fishing excursion he had planned for the next morning. All the harder to trace, he figured. Despite his normally bold demeanor, Cemanski was cautious not to be followed. He had learned to watch his tail back in the years when the county government was looking for any reason they could find to outlaw his preservation society.

Jason McAlpin arrived next, followed shortly by Robert Sonnvoldt and his passenger, Tamara Hopkins. The five governing members of the Land Preservation Society were now convened.

Tom directed the vehicles to a drive that wrapped around the side of his garage to the rear of his residence. The neighbors across the street were accustomed to seeing visitors at the Sanders' home so they wouldn't be suspicious but Tom wasn't taking chances. He didn't want to leave the vehicles out front where the wrong person might have time to study the license tags.

The Sanders owned a large brick home set at the front of an eighty-acre parcel of land perched on what otherwise had become a residential street. A beautifully maintained fruit tree orchard also ran along the front-side of the large lot. Towards the rear, the property was bordered on two sides by a bend in the Rock River. The land sloped sharply and formed a bluff overlooking the river on the western edge of the property. It was just before the bluff, as the land began to slope, where one of the few examples of terraced farming in the State of Illinois could be found. This was the feature that enabled Sanders to acquire the property to begin with. As Professor of Agrarian History at Northern Illinois University, Sanders was able to convince the government that the property should be held in his hands in order to facilitate further study.

Sanders doubted that he would have been able to do the same bit of convincing today. Older residents remembered Ogle County as being in the heart of the most fertile farmland in America. But as each year passed, the formerly sleepy borough covering almost a half a million acres was considered more and more a part of metropolitan Chicago with its downtown located some ninety miles to the east. Then after the county lost its "Semi-Rural" status, local government didn't hold much regard for agrarian history. Even in the year when he purchased the land it had been no easy transaction. It helped that his wife, Marina, was an up and coming attorney in Ogle County. She was able to maneuver through the various obstacles the government had established. In addition, her handsome income helped finance the purchase.

Marina Sanders completely supported the efforts of the Land Preservation Society. But given her high profile position she felt that it was best that she wasn't a member and didn't participate in the group's activities. That way she could truthfully deny her involvement with, or knowledge of, the society's activities. This was often to Tom's chagrin because he would have appreciated her guidance at many a council meeting but, overall, he too agreed that it would be best that Marina remain uninvolved. Not surprisingly though, over the time since her husband had joined the group Marina gradually grew more acquainted with them and couldn't help but give each council member a warm greeting as Tom ushered them through the back door and into their den. She assured that they were comfortable and insisted on finding each their favorite drink before excusing herself from their meeting.

Marina had hardly closed the door before Andy Cemanski started the meeting with a scolding. "Robert, did you really find it necessary to give Tamara a ride here tonight?"

"Well yes," Robert replied. "We figured that'd give them chances of spotting one less of our vehicles this evening."

"Great!" Cemanski recoiled. "So if they happen to place surveillance on one of the winning bidders, then what to their surprise but he just happens to go pick up another one."

It had become no secret among the council members that Robert and Tamara had developed something more than just a professional relationship. But they had all agreed that as long as their relationship didn't compromise the mission of the society, then there was no issue.

"We're not that stupid, Andy," Robert objected. "Tamara took a walk from her town home. She stopped at a restaurant for a bite to eat. I was able to pick her up from there without anyone noticing."

"So how do you plan to get her home, young man?" Andy snapped.

"Okay, your point is well taken," Tom interrupted. "We need to be very careful. I hope each of us understands the importance of that. So now let's get down to business and talk about what we've learned from the auction."

After Andy and Robert cooled off Jason started the discussion by saying, "First, we learned what shrewd bidding agents we have amongst us."

"Yes, of course," Sanders said as he nodded in the direction of a table adjacent to a stone fireplace in one corner of the room. "Congratulations are in order and there just happens to be a chilled bottle of champagne sitting right over there."

Sanders stood and walked to the table to fill five glasses. When each member of the society's governing council held a glass, Tom toasted, "Here is to Mr. Sonnvoldt and here is to Ms. Hopkins, even if she did blatantly exceed our budget." Tom winked and then added, "They walked into the lion's den and secured their quarry."

Andy chimed in begrudgingly trying to forgive Robert and Tamara for the carelessness they demonstrated by riding together to Sanders' home. "Also here is to the society, which has saved," he hesitated, "for now anyway, two hundred acres of land."

They all took a drink of champagne and then Tom said in a serious tone, "I think we'll be okay for awhile with the northwest property. But I don't know how long it'll be before Tamara starts to receive pressure from the county to see more detail on her development plans. Gardner will try to force the OLM to make her show her hand. The property is right in the midst of several GDC projects."

"Don't worry." Tamara said. "I'm sure we'll figure out a plan to stall them," she added as she turned away and glanced toward the window.

"Yes," Sanders said inquiringly noticing Tamara's subtle body language. "I am sure that, together, we can all come up with a plan to delay any development on that property."

Then, Sanders placed a surveying eye to the other council members. "However," he said, "first, we must redirect ourselves to the primary purpose of our activities at the auction. Who did we see and what did we learn of their complicities? Why don't you start, Andy? You were right there in the pits."

"Well, as always," Cemanski started, "there never seems to be a shortage of unsavory, money grubbing characters at such events. However, the bigwigs decided to be more visual than usual."

"Yes," Robert added. "John Gardner was strutting around with an air of superiority. It was rather pleasant to see him get agitated when he lost those two properties right there on Prairie Parkway."

"Certainly was, but I wasn't all that surprised by Gardner's behavior," Andy retorted. "What shocked me was when Sir Arthur himself came through the door. Flemming has developed most of DeKalb County and what was left of Kane County. For some reason, though, he's never seemed that interested in our county. That is until he came in and outbid Gardner for the big parcel on Prairie Parkway. It was nice to see Gardner get knocked down a peg, but don't be misled. Flemming may seem more refined, but he's just as much the blood sucking bastard that Gardner is."

Andy had some not so fond memories of Arthur Flemming. Flemming was quite a bit younger, no older than Andy's son; however, the two had engaged in a few fierce battles over property rights. Flemming had mastered the art of land acquisition at an early age. He rarely confronted his opposition head on, but he was skilled at the arts of deception and legal technicalities. Unquestionably, the LPS lost the war in Kane and DeKalb Counties and some insist that it was Arthur Flemming who plunged the final sword through their heart.

"I don't know what to make of these developer rivalries yet," Tom Sanders commented. "But what about the politicians? Did anyone see them lurking about?"

"As a matter of fact, yes," Jason McAlpin piped in. "I was watching Gardner enjoy his breakfast at the Greenery before the auction when who should stop in to say hello? It was none other than our number one county official."

They all knew that McAlpin was referring to Nathan Coulter, the County Clerk. In Ogle County, the County Clerk was the highest office.

McAlpin continued, "It was all very casual. Just glad-handing, which isn't unusual for either Gardner or Coulter. I didn't think much of it until I talked to my daughter later about what she saw at the Rexford. And now, after what Andy's said, it makes me think even more."

"You had your daughter stake out the Rexford?" Tamara asked with surprise.

"Um, yeah," Jason answered sheepishly.

Jennifer had taken a job at the Hotel at her father's request. She was still working her way through college and she shared her father's passion for land preservation. When she was younger, Jason obtained the necessary permits to take Jennifer and her brothers camping at some of the national parks. By the time she reached her teens, Jennifer and her dad had already had several discussions concerning the Nation's need to do a better job at preserving land. They chatted about the liberating affect that open country had on one's character. However, never had she suspected that her father was an active member in an organization fighting to protect the very dreams they discussed. Then, when he asked her to observe the goings on at the Rexford before the auction in order that she might help in the cause for land preservation she was more than eager to assist.

Tom Sanders was uncomfortable when McAlpin brought forth his plan to have his daughter stake out the Rexford Hotel. However, Jason assured him that Jennifer had not been made aware of the LPS's overall activities or, for that matter, even the name of the society or identity of any of its members. So Tom agreed to overlook the risk and accept the help. Besides, despite the secretive nature of the LPS, Tom knew that the society's ultimate success depended on the recruitment of additional members including an emphasis toward younger members.

What McAlpin's daughter relayed to him on the day of the auction was that she saw the County Clerk enter the lobby of the Rexford Hotel at ten minutes after nine. This, of course, was after the auction had already started at the county building across the street.

"Jennifer told me that Nathan Coulter came in with one of his aides. He looked around and then took a seat in the lobby. He sat for about a minute before he began looking at his watch and seeming to become anxious. Finally, an important looking man exited from the elevator and came over to meet with Coulter."

"Who was it?" Andy asked.

"Well, she said that she didn't recognize the man. However, she's a sharp girl. She brought me an image of the registry, which contained the names of all the hotel's guests. Given that information and the description of the man, I have to deduce that it could have been but one person."

"Well," Andy implored.

"It had to be Arthur Flemming."

"Flemming?" Robert questioned. "So the County Clerk met with Gardner and Flemming that morning. Do you think they're all in cahoots?"

"Doubtful," Andy responded. "I can't imagine that three egos that large would work very well together. My guess would be that Coulter is playing the two off of each other and waiting to see who can pad his pockets the most. We just need to uncover a credible link that we can use to expose him."

"Interesting. Did you see anything from your post?" Robert directed at Tom.

"Not much," Tom answered without elaborating.

What Tom chose not to tell the council is what he had seen earlier on the morning of the auction, before he had reached his post. Tom drove his rental vehicle down various streets in the vicinity of the county building that morning. He was taking the chance, hoping that he might spot something out of the ordinary. That's when he noticed Tamara's vehicle parked at a convenience store some three blocks from the county building. He watched, waiting for her to come out of the store. Finally, before this happened, a limousine pulled up next to where she had parked. The rear door of the larger vehicle opened and, to Tom's surprise, Tamara got out. She left the door open long enough while making a parting comment to give Tom an opportunity to see the other passenger in the back seat. It was Arthur Flemming.

Tom Sanders was stunned by what he had witnessed, but nevertheless he chose not to mention it that evening. He had always respected Tamara and had never doubted her loyalty to the society. He hoped that Tamara would volunteer an explanation for her rendezvous with Flemming before he couldn't wait any longer and felt compelled to demand an answer.

# Chapter 5

Saturday evening while the LPS was meeting at the home of Thomas Sanders; John Gardner paid a visit to the County Clerk's apartment. Nathan Coulter's apartment occupied the entire upper floor of a seven-story building in the heart of Ogletown, the county seat. The building towered over the surrounding structures and from the rooftop patio Coulter could gaze out upon his burgeoning municipality. Except for the ornate county building just a few blocks away, there were only nondescript residences and commercial outlets to be seen sprawling into the distance street after street. It was to this rooftop that Coulter hurriedly rushed Gardner when he arrived.

"Nancy is in the bedroom getting dressed for our evening appointments. I hope you don't mind, John, but I'd prefer that she didn't know that you stopped by."

"That's fine, Nate," Gardner replied. "I don't plan to take up much of your time. I was just hoping that you could explain a few things to me."

"I don't ever remember having to explain anything to John Gardner. Sounds like I better get you a Scotch. It is still Scotch that you drink?" Coulter asked as he made his way to the bar at the far end of the rooftop pool.

"Of course," Gardner replied, without emotion, as he followed Coulter to the bar.

Coulter surveyed the shelves to the rear of the well-stocked bar and, then, pulled down an unopened bottle of aged Scotch. He opened the bottle and filled two small tumblers to near their brims. He raised one of the glasses and announced, "This is to John Gardner."

Coulter paused after swallowing the contents of half his glass before saying, "Now, how can I help you?"

John Gardner was a naturally aggressive man, normally taking no time to get to his point. However, as he aged, he had trained himself to display more patience, particularly when he was dealing with refined politicians. So Gardner delayed answering Coulter's question. First, he raised his drink and declared, "This is to Nathan Coulter."

Then, Gardner placed his glass down and said, "I was hoping that you could explain a few things that happened at the auction the other day."

"I wasn't there but I'll try to answer whatever I can for you."

Gardner ignored Coulter's patronizing tone and said, "There were a few unexpected guests in the crowd."

"Yes, I understand that there were two new bidders who were awarded properties."

"I'm not worried about them," Gardner shot back. "I was actually referring to a much more well known face. Someone who is very familiar to us both; however, who I wouldn't expect to appear at an Ogle County auction."

"Are you referring to Arthur Flemming?"

"You know I'm talking about Flemming, Nate."

"Well, what do you want me to tell you?"

"Nate, I try to be a very reasonable man. I don't mind opening the floor to a few new bidders every once in a while. I cooperate with the other developers in this county. It's good for business. It would probably even get a little boring if GDC were the only ones bidding on anything around here. You know I've even forced myself to tolerate those clowns over at Cranstead."

"That's good of you, John. But when is it that you're going to tell me what I can help you with?" Coulter began to grow irritated perhaps sensing that Gardner mimicked the same sort of patronizing tone that he often found himself employing.

"I want you to explain how it is that I didn't know that Arthur Flemming was going to be at the auction!" Gardner asked irreverently instantly switching back to his more natural demeanor.

"Come now, John, don't tell me you've lost your touch. Your people didn't read the registry? It was right there to see that Pinnacle Development was signed in for a bidding seat."

"Yes they've been known to do that occasionally," Gardner countered. "He'll send a couple of toads over to stick their nose into our county's business. They come just to check out what we're up to. But, when was the last time that Arthur Flemming stepped foot over here? I think his presence was a sure sign that Pinnacle had a keen interest in something over here. Why didn't you tell me that he was going to show up? What's he up to?"

"What should I know of Flemming's business?" Coulter responded coolly.

"You were seen meeting with him that morning. You didn't care to mention that to me when you saw me at the Greenery?"

"I'm a public official. It's my job to meet with people. I'm meeting here with you, aren't I?"

"Yes, but of course you don't want your wife to know that I'm here."

"Touché, Mr. Gardner. The visit with Flemming was a courtesy call. There's really nothing more to tell you."

Gardner didn't respond immediately. He gazed around at the patio and out to the shimmering lights below. "This is really a beautiful place you have here, Nate. No doubt that this must be the nicest apartment in town. How many people have a rooftop swimming pool? GDC did a fine job at constructing this building. Oh, and the furnishings you've added are a fine touch. You and your wife have exquisite taste, Nate. We don't really get involved with the furnishing business, ourselves. However, in an indirect way, I guess you could say that GDC helped you acquire these as well. Working with GDC has really been pretty good for you, hasn't it Nate?"

Gardner paused only briefly so as not to give Coulter time to respond to what was a rhetorical question. He continued, "I was saying before that a little competition is good. But please note my emphasis on the word, little. A lot of competition is not so good. Okay, so maybe in the short run you'd be flattered with all the attention you get. But, believe me, in the long run it would not be so good for you, Nate. Humans are jealous creatures by nature. Whoever is on the losing side might not be happy with how well you live here. It's probably best that you don't let the competition get too big of a taste of how it feels to win in this county."

Coulter stared back at Gardner seemingly unfazed by what he had heard. "Are you through, John?"

Earlier in his career, as Coulter was making his way up the ladder of county government, he might have felt threatened by Gardner's remarks. But Nate Coulter had become a powerful man and no longer did such words disquiet him, for the Clerk had more control over almost every facet of county life than anyone had ever had before.

Some twenty years ago, top county officials throughout the nation had gained substantial strength when the United States legislature had approved the President's County Designation Plan. Ever since, county officials continued to gain authority while state governments were rendered increasingly irrelevant. In many states the governor had less influence than a strong county clerk.

The County Designation Plan was originally seen as a drastic measure by the federal government to control the haphazard suburban sprawl continuing to canvass the nation. The government believed the Plan essential toward placing order to growth and to saving what remained of the nation's agricultural land and wilderness marvels. Greed had spoiled all state and local government as well as private sector plans to save the country's landscape. Eventually the federal government was pressured to step in.

When the County Designation Plan was enacted there was a fairly vociferous public cry that the government had gone too far. However, as the years passed there were more and more people who felt that the Plan had not gone nearly far enough.

Under the Plan every county in the nation had been assigned a label under six broad categories. The categories initially enacted remained: 1) Industrial, 2) Residential, 3) Mixed–Business and Residential, by far the most common designation, 4) Agricultural, 5) Semi-Rural and 6) Wilderness. Only the United States Congress was granted authority to change a county's designation. But each county's local government assumes sole responsibility for controlling development and land use in accordance with the designation received and under federal Plan guidelines.

It was the County Designation Plan coupled with Nathan Coulter's shrewd political savvy that enabled him to usurp the power that he enjoyed. So now Coulter exercised his prerogative to disregard the hand that the normally influential developer was trying to play. Instead he just glared at Gardner who stood nearly a foot taller than the stubby politician. They remained locked in silence for several moments until finally being interrupted by a call from the stairs. "Honey, are you up there? I'm ready to…"

"Yes, dear," Coulter called back toward the stairs. "I'll be right down."

"Well, John, I've enjoyed our little talk," Coulter said turning back to face Gardner. "However as you just heard, it's time for me to attend to my appointments. But since it's such a beautiful summer evening, feel free to pour yourself another drink and enjoy the breeze from up here. My aide is still working downstairs and he can lock up behind you when you're ready to leave."

With that Coulter headed to the staircase while Gardner remained behind adjusting his stiff posture and leaning forward to rest up against the bar. As Coulter descended the steps Gardner's direct link device vibrated. "Hello," Gardner answered expecting to hear from one of his lieutenants on the other end.

It was the man Gardner had instructed to tail Tamara Hopkins. "I have some interesting news," he said.

"Go on."

"Ms. Hopkins was picked up this evening by the fellow who made the ancestral claim at the auction."

"Hopkins was picked up by the farmer? What was his name again?"

"Robert Sonnvoldt, sir."

"Sonnvoldt. Yes that name sounds vaguely familiar," Gardner replied.

"Yeah, who would have guessed that they were even acquainted? However, by the way he greeted her I'd say that they're quite familiar with one another. Do you know what I mean, boss?"

"Yes. Where did they go?"

"They headed away from downtown toward the river. They ended up at the house of some people who own quite a bit of land. I did some checking and found out the property is registered to Thomas and Marina Sanders. Thomas is a professor at Northern Illinois University and Marina is a lawyer."

"Did anyone else come to the house?"

"I couldn't tell. There weren't any other vehicles in the driveway. However, when Hopkins and Sonnvoldt arrived a man came out to meet them. I assume that it must have been Sanders. He had them pull around the side of the garage to the back. So who knows, there could've been more vehicles parked back there?"

"Okay, stay there until they leave. See if anyone else comes out of the house."

"I can't because I already left. The neighbors across the road kept peeking out the window at me. They looked all suspicious and stuff."

Gardner let out an irritable sigh. "Okay then, find out more about the professor and also see what you can learn about farmer Romeo. Find out how long he and Lady Hopkins have been together. I'll meet with you tomorrow."

After Gardner clicked off his link he reached for the bottle of Scotch and filled his glass three quarters to the top. He lifted the tumbler to his lips and swigged down its contents in one gulp. Then, he made his way down from the patio into the main apartment where he declared in a voice loud enough to be heard by Coulter's aide, "I'm leaving now."

Coulter's aide, Clayton Addison, waited to hear the door open and shut before he switched off the intercom in the study where he had been listening to the rooftop conversation.

"How interesting," Addison muttered and then went to make sure that Gardner had gone.

"It always helps to have a second set of ears to understand what really is being said," Coulter had told his aide before Gardner had arrived. "So listen in on what he has to tell me." Hardly did Addison expect to hear more conversation once his boss had departed and left Gardner alone on the rooftop.

# Chapter 6

Arthur Flemming clearly remembered his first encounter with Tamara Hopkins. She was a teenager working part-time at her parent's development company. Flemming had come to discuss a business transaction with her parents when he saw her there working behind the front desk.

Flemming recollected walking in and introducing himself to the receptionist who was a very pretty girl but quite young. At the time, Flemming was a rather young businessman himself no more than in his late twenties. He told the girl he was there to see both Mr. and Mrs. Hopkins.

"Please take a seat," the young lady smiled. "I'll let the Hopkins know that you are here."

"That's all right, they're expecting me. I can make my way back on my own," Flemming responded.

"Please, sir, take a seat. I'd prefer to ring their office to announce your arrival first."

"Don't bother, miss," he said as he nonchalantly sauntered by the front desk.

Arthur Flemming had worked for the Hopkins several years previously right after graduating from college. He considered the experience his first, and only other, real job. Ambition got the best of him and he hadn't worked for the Hopkins for very long before venturing out to start his own development company. Arthur was very successful and in short order his business had grown to be larger than that of the Hopkins. Nevertheless, he remained close to the couple and continued to request their counsel oftentimes only as an excuse to come over for a chat. As a result, he still felt at home when he came to their offices and thought nothing of finding his own way back to see the Hopkins unescorted. The young receptionist thought otherwise.

When Flemming passed her desk she sprang to her feet and hurried after him. She caught the businessman about halfway down the hall and grabbed his arm firmly. "Sir, I really don't want you going back there until I've had a chance to introduce you. Please return to the lobby and have a seat."

Flemming was a tall man and he towered over the young receptionist both in physical and business stature. His immediate thoughts were is she nuts and does she have any idea what she is doing? She didn't let go of his arm, however, and it must have been the look she gave him that made Flemming realize that it was he who was in the wrong. He was behaving with an air of self-importance while this young lady was just trying to do her job. He sensed her conviction; she was fearless.

"You're right, miss. I should return to the lobby."

It wasn't until later, when he complimented them on the dedication of their receptionist, that Flemming learned that Tamara was the Hopkins' daughter. Flemming encountered Tamara just twice subsequent to their initial acquaintance, but both instances further reinforced the impression she had made. She's the type of person I'd like to hire to work at my shop, he thought.

Now, much more recently, Tamara Hopkins came to mind again. Flemming's Pinnacle Development staff was discussing the pros and cons of increasing their presence in Ogle County. Pinnacle was still the largest developer but their growth opportunities were coming harder to find and the company was less aggressive than it had been in the past. A faction of the management team was eager to become more active and Ogle County seemed like a natural possibility for expansion. They discussed potential roadblocks to entering the area and besides obvious competition from GDC and certain other developers, one manager brought up the possible resistance from the Land Preservation Society.

"The LPS," another manager scoffed. "Nathan Coulter had them banned from the county years ago."

"Yes, maybe so, but the word is that they're making a comeback."

"Who's their leader?"

"Some say Andy Cemanski," the manager replied. "That seems doubtful though. He's probably as cantankerous as ever, but his glory days have passed him by and I can't see him rallying the troops anymore. They're probably afraid he'd lead them straight to jail."

"Who else then is part of this alleged LPS?"

A few members of the management team who kept a loose eye on anti-development activists threw out some names, one of which caught Arthur Flemming's ear.

"Tamara Hopkins runs a consulting business," the manager who brought up the issue stated. "However, we've connected her with several environmental movements and have a credible source linking her to the LPS."

Of course, Flemming thought when he heard her name. Flemming still talked to her parents on rare occasion and based on the little things they said about Tamara it didn't surprise him at all that she might become involved with a group like the LPS. When he had inquired about a succession plan for their business they responded, "Tamara said she wouldn't dream of taking over the company. She said she'd prefer to be in the business of putting developers out of business. Tamara's been a wonderful daughter, but by the time she was off to college she'd already made it clear that she didn't care for the profession we had chosen." There were other comments the Hopkins' had made as well, but for now Flemming remained silent. He chose to make no mention to his team that he had ever met Tamara Hopkins.

However, as his subordinates continued to discuss the LPS, Flemming was beginning to formulate a plan. Just possibly, Tamara could create the perfect diversion and serve to reintroduce him to Ogle County. Perhaps she could distract John Gardner long enough to provide him the opportunity to extract a few parcels of land from GDC's hands. So the next day Flemming placed a call to the offices of Tamara Hopkins' consulting firm. After skillfully cajoling her secretary to patch him through he asked Tamara if she could find time to meet for lunch sometime soon.

"Whatever for?" Tamara heard herself saying before having the chance to filter through to a more subtle response. Tamara couldn't help herself; she despised Flemming. Perhaps her particular memory of the incident was more vague, but she also remembered the first encounter between herself and Arthur Flemming. She recalled his arrogance but that wasn't what really bothered her. The key factor was that Arthur Flemming was the head of a major development firm. She had learned to loathe all developers and was thrilled when her parents finally decided to close down their development company.

"I've heard that you run a very successful consulting practice and I just thought that Pinnacle Development, or myself personally, could benefit from your counsel," Flemming explained.

"Thank you for the kind words, Mr. Flemming. However, our firm doesn't provide services to either the real estate or development industry. I doubt that we could be of any help to you."

"Please, call me Arthur, and I think you're being a bit too modest, Tamara. Your parents had told me that you gathered a remarkably quick understanding of the development industry in the short time that you worked for them. They said that you could have easily taken over the business for them and likely would have improved it and grown it."

Yes, thought Tamara, how fortunate that my parents came to their senses and got out of that godforsaken business. She would be no legacy to its sins. So Flemming's flattery failed to affect he; however, he had played the 'parent card' and for some reason her parents had always liked Arthur Flemming. For their sake then, she felt that she probably owed the man the courtesy of one visit.

Tamara gazed through her calendar and finally said, "Next Tuesday would work for lunch. However, Arthur, I must tell you that we're really not taking any new business right now."

Flemming and Hopkins met for lunch and made small talk and reconnected on their brief history together. Arthur told her, " The day you pulled me back into the lobby was a revelation for me. It helped me start considering the other person's point of view." He's more gracious than I would have imagined, Tamara thought as she listened. He's not quite the conceited, young businessman that I recollected. Flemming, though still tall and athletic looking, appeared more distinguished and his temples were beginning to gray. He spoke eloquently in a soft tone.

"Let me just say that I have good reason to believe that you're not very fond of us developer-types," he continued. "My senses tell me that you wouldn't even have agreed to meet if it weren't for my association with your parents. However, I think that given a chance, you may come to find that my views are not all that different from yours."

Flemming's perception about her dislike for developers was right on, but how had he picked up on that already? Perhaps her feelings were even more transparent than she had thought or maybe her parents had become more comfortable discussing her environmental activism as the years passed? They probably told him something about me, but they would have never told him that I'm with the LPS. Regardless, she felt the need to challenge his last comment. There seemed to be no way that their views on land preservation could be similar. "Well, Arthur, I think a person's views are normally reflected in the actions they take. And I think it is safe to say that the actions you've taken over the years are quite different than the ones I've taken."

"Agreed," Arthur responded. Recognizing that he wasn't going to win Tamara over on broad philosophical terms in just one visit, he paused before moving on to the specifics of his plan. "I can help you acquire a parcel of land and keep it out of the hands of GDC," he declared. "Then,

I'll use your purchase as the cornerstone to allow me to acquire additional properties and keep them from being developed by GDC."

Since Flemming already knew her feelings toward developers there was no sense in holding back and so she responded, "How do I know that your intentions for the property are any better than those of John Gardner?"

"Right now you don't. Trust can only be developed over time. However, after we're finished, at a minimum, at least you'll own some prime acreage right in the heart of Ogle County."

After further discussion, Tamara agreed to consider Arthur's plan when they parted the restaurant. Arthur watched her as she walked to her vehicle. What an intelligent, attractive woman she had become. He thought how the passage of years had the effect of narrowing their age difference. Also, as a single man by way of divorce, he couldn't help but to wish that their meeting could have been for something more than purely business purposes.

Tamara and Arthur met several more times to discuss the plan to acquire land in Ogle County. Their final meeting was that very morning before the auction when Tom Sanders was shocked when he saw them together at the convenience store just a few blocks from the county building.

# Chapter 7

The private roadway leading into Gardner Development Company curved around a small lake highlighted by an ornate Romanesque fountain in its center. The offices at the end of the drive were set in a well-constructed, two-story brick building. Larger limestone blocks were purposely set in an uneven pattern over the bricks near the building's corners. The structure had a stately appeal, reminiscent of architecture prominent some two to three hundred years previously, which belied its modern inside décor and function.

John Gardner stopped his vehicle under the front portico at eleven a.m., which was precisely the time he told his officers and key aides when he would arrive. Their five vehicles were already parked in the executive lot to the side of the main entrance. Gardner walked directly to the lone limestone block near the front entry and waved his hand across a barely visible scanner embedded in the stone. The doors slid open and he quickly made his way through the foyer and down the hall.

By the time he reached the first floor conference room he was beaming. "Good morning," he greeted his assembled staff. "I'm glad everyone could make it on such short notice."

Most of the staff members just nodded. All of them had been there since before eight. They were accustomed to and complied with Gardner's "whatever it takes" attitude. That was how they had rose through the ranks at GDC and they were well compensated for it.

The Chief Information Officer couldn't resist chiding her boss, however. "My husband is a little upset, John. Missing church services again, you know. He thinks I'm becoming a heathen."

"Maybe next week, Cristin," Gardner responded. "This is important."

Gardner surveyed his staff again to make sure all were present. In addition to Cristin Anelli, his Operations Director, his Financial Officer,

Communications Director, who also served as his public bidding agent, and Lucas Mason were all there. No one could ever remember the title Gardner gave Lucas. They usually referred to him as the "Right Hand." Mason was the one who had followed Tamara Hopkins the previous night.

"I wasn't happy when I saw Arthur Flemming at the auction last week," Gardner resumed. "So last night I attempted to see if our illustrious County Clerk could explain why Pinnacle was there. But Mr. Coulter decided to play coy. He seems to have temporarily forgotten all of the favors we've provided for him. He'll come around though. He always has. In the meantime, we'll have to take care of matters for ourselves. This is our county and we won't stand for Pinnacle trying to take any of it away from us.

'The first thing we're going to do is reclaim the eighty acres on Prairie Parkway that, let's just say, we let the Hopkins woman temporarily borrow. Then, we'll pinch off Pinnacle's property and isolate them before they have any thoughts about growing here."

Gardner paused to let his objectives sink in with his staff. He walked slowly to the small table set in one corner of the room and poured a cup of coffee before continuing.

"It was quite a surprise when Lucas called last night to tell me that Ms. Hopkins is cavorting with the farmer. That gives us an opportunity to exploit and should make completing the first part of our job rather simple. But I'd also like to know if the connection with this Sanders fellow has any importance. Has anyone learned anything?"

"On first blush they seem to make a rather odd group," Cristin answered first. "We have a business consultant, a farmstead claimant and a professor. However, I think I've found at least one connection."

Cristin Anelli was a master at discovering information on not only properties but people as well. For one thing, she had direct access to the county database. Something the county never bothered to block in return for a political favor from GDC. She would have easily found a new way into the database anyway just as she had found her way into hundreds of others. Her real talent, however, was her ability to filter and organize the information that she found. There were many researchers who could locate data, but sheer volume made it difficult for them to make sense of what was found, particularly when it came to linking objects such as people with other objects. Anelli had the innate ability to connect these links.

"The connection is?"

"Tamara Hopkins was in Paris eleven years ago and registered for a conference on land use and preservation at the Sorbonne. You know how the Europeans think that they have all these sacred grounds that they need to protect. Well, it so happens, that Professor Thomas Sanders was one of the speakers at the conference. Sanders who was in his thirties at the time gave a dissertation entitled, 'The Sociological Benefits of Maintaining Rural Communities: An American Perspective."

"What was Ms. Hopkins involvement in the conference?" Gardner inquired.

"I'm not sure. She was a 'walk-up', registering on the first morning of the conference."

"How do you find all this?" the financial officer asked in puzzled amazement.

"French history, my dear. They can't seem to purge any of their records," Anelli replied smugly.

"Couldn't it have been coincidental that she was there when he happened to be speaking?" he followed.

"Perhaps or even probably, but the young Miss Hopkins must have been moved by the dashing professor's presentation. What followed can hardly be coincidental. That fall when Hopkins returned from her European sabbatical she signed up for Professor Sanders' agrarian history class at Northern Illinois University. That seems to be a rather unusual subject for a law student, particularly one who was enrolled at a different university."

"Are there any other connections between them?" Gardner asked.

"No. Not until last night anyway when Lucas saw her visit Sanders' home."

Anelli was correct in her assumption that Tamara did not register for Professor Sanders' class by accident. When Tamara attended the Sorbonne conference eleven years ago Sanders' talk helped her round out an already strong belief in the need to save wild areas, rural areas and open space in general. Tamara was moved by his passion for land preservation and his ability to connect it to the human psyche. The professor was able to explain how land preservation went beyond saving nature for nature's sake. Existence in a more natural, balanced world was essential for saving an inherent part of the human soul. Sanders provided the words to describe her feelings.

Being so moved by Sanders' speech she approached him after the conference. She told them that she grew up in northern Illinois fairly close to the university where he taught and then she asked if he was a member of the LPS. Tamara herself had become a member the previous year.

"No miss, I'm not familiar with the LPS. Is that an acronym for something?"

"Yes, it stands for Land Preservation Society. I just thought that given your obvious passion for conservation you might be affiliated with the society."

"I'm involved with a few organizations but I don't know anything about the LPS."

At the time, the LPS was a much more radical society than any organization to which Sanders was referring. The LPS was formed years before the federal government enacted the County Designation Plan. Chapters were started in various parts of the country in an attempt to stem the tide of residential and commercial developments washing over U.S. soil. The LPS exposed corrupt developers and municipal officials and they employed various methods to raise the public's awareness of unsound development practices from ad campaigns, sit-ins and protests to, at the height of the movement, violence. Then when local politicians gained more power after the County Designation Plan many counties began to outlaw the LPS while the federal government remained silent regarding this encroachment on civil liberties. Federal powerbrokers chose to cater to the development industry and the perceived economic rewards that it provided and rested their environmental laurels on the County Designation Plan. As a result, many chapters of the LPS were abandoned and those that remained went underground as independent splinter groups.

Since the LPS was already becoming a secretive society by the time they met, even if the professor had been a member, it was doubtful he would have told Tamara on occasion of their first acquaintance. However, Tamara sensed he was being honest and that he really didn't know anything about the society. Oh but, with his knowledge and passion, what a valuable member he would make, she thought. That's why Tamara enrolled in his class when she got back to the States. The student was going to go about recruiting the teacher. The recruitment process actually went on for several years before the professor was finally convinced that he should join the LPS.

John Gardner was mildly impressed by Cristin Anelli's ability to connect Hopkins to Sanders via their land preservation interests. "Perhaps Hopkins and her farmer friend went to see Sanders for advice on preserving the eighty acres she bought. That property is still a cornfield you know," Gardner said. However, having been researching for only three hours, Anelli had yet to uncover the trio's leadership positions on the LPS council. As a result, Gardner chose to lead his team's attack in a different direction. "I'm not sure how the Sanders relationship helps us," he said. "Tell me more about the farmer."

"His name is Robert Sonnvoldt," Cristin answered.

"Julie, you saw him at the auction," Gardner stated looking toward his Communications Director. "Did you have any idea that he and Hopkins were together?"

"No idea," Dubose responded. "I never saw them make eye contact. I never saw them near each other. She came across as this cool, professional woman. He, on the other hand, didn't look like he belonged in the building. He certainly played the part of a farmer."

"And I think it really was a play," Cristin Anelli interjected. "There's a little more to Mr. Sonnvoldt than he let on. He was not always a so-called 'farmsteader'. He was in the insurance business. He operated his own agency for a while until he sold it, for a fairly hefty sum I might add."

John Gardner contemplated the additional information for a few moments and then instructed, "Go get the land back from Sonnvoldt next week."

"The property he purchased up in the northwest sector?" the operations director inquired.

"No, get the land that Hopkins purchased."

"I'm a little confused, John. Why do you want us to go to Sonnvoldt then?"

"I think we need to exploit this girlfriend-boyfriend angle. Julie, I want you to pay a visit to Mr. Sonnvoldt. Request that he convince Ms. Hopkins to sell her eighty acres back to us. Tell him that if he does this we might be able to get him a few additional acres out in the northwest sector, something he and his girlfriend can sink their preservationist teeth into."

"What if Sonnvoldt can't convince Hopkins to sell?"

"That's when Lucas will have to get involved."

"How so, boss?" Lucas inquired.

"If Julie can't gently persuade the man, take a few of your men over to explain the risk his girlfriend faces if she decides not to sell. Sonnvoldt was in the insurance business so he should understand the importance of protecting against risk."

# Chapter 8

"Honey, you've hardly said a word all morning," Marina Sanders told her husband as they were finishing their Sunday brunch.

"I'm sorry. I guess I've had a lot on my mind."

"Well, tell me what it is, maybe I can help."

"I'll be all right, it's really nothing."

"Society business," Marina deduced.

"Sort of."

The society was their barrier to complete openness with one another. Marina was supportive and even curious about what Tom was up to with the LPS but she never asked, at least not directly. Sometimes the secret society created tension between them, but the overriding strength of their relationship squelched any lingering anxiety.

"I'm going for a walk out back," Tom said hoping to snap his dour mood.

"Okay, but please be back by noon. Don't forget we have Colleen's voice recital."

"Of course," Tom called as he headed out the back door.

Colleen was thirteen and their only child. She had beautiful dark eyes like her mother, but her father's fair complexion. She was born after the Sanders were into their thirties and had been married a number of years. As a result, the couple had to make adjustments to their busy, career-oriented lifestyles but the changes were welcomed. Tom was there for every voice recital, dance recital, school play, soccer game and baseball game. He car-pooled for Colleen and her friends, helped with her homework and surprised her with little gifts. The constant doting hadn't turned Colleen into the "spoiled only child." She was well adjusted and took on the even temperament of both parents.

But on this day, Tom was out the door no more than ten steps before he forgot all about Colleen's recital. He'd been troubled ever since the morning of the auction and last night he had hoped Tamara would have put his concern to rest by telling the council what she had been doing with Arthur Flemming.

As he consternated, Tom followed a path through a well-manicured orchard of apple and pear trees. Tom had never questioned Tamara's judgment before. She was young and impetuous when he met her in Paris but even then he had sensed her underlying intellect and insightfulness. Now, at their society meetings, he often counted on her to sway the council to the side of reason. She helped calm Andy Cemanski who in many instances still resorted to taking the most direct path without regard to consequence. And of course Tamara held influence over Robert Sonnvoldt. Robert was cut from a different cloth yet seemed determined to be Andy's protégé and he could get excitable at times, until Tamara put the clamps on him.

As to Tamara's loyalty Tom had never placed that in question either. Andy and Robert may have been more vocal and blustery but in her more pragmatic manner she was just as convicted to land preservation as they were. After all, wasn't it Tamara who had recruited Tom to the LPS?

Why would Tamara associate with Arthur Flemming, a man responsible for destroying countless acres of land? Had Flemming bought Tamara; was it greed? Instead, was it fear, Tom wondered. Had Flemming threatened her? Tom hoped that there was a better explanation than any he'd considered so far.

As Sanders continued down the path, the uniformity of the orchard gave way to a mixed forest of oak, maple and pine covering ten acres of land near the center of the property. The woods and a somewhat smaller prairie clearing beyond the trees were Tom's favorite places. They provided a sublime, wilder respite from his generally suburban surroundings. These were forbidden grounds, however, because the deed to Sanders' property restricted land use under his ownership to the historical study of terraced cropland and orchards. The forest and prairie had been overlooked on the survey and no one knew that it was really this small patch of wild land that drove Sanders' desire to obtain the property.

When he reached the prairie Tom could see beyond to the top of the cornfield before it sloped down to the river. When he brought official visitors to observe the terraced fields he never took them on this path. They were always driven along the access road on the southern edge of the property.

It was in the middle of the prairie where, while still thinking about Tamara, his curiosity finally conquered his patience. He clutched his tiny direct link device and placed the call.

"Hi Tom," she responded somewhat surprised to hear from him.

"Sorry to bother you but there's something I need to ask you."

"What is it?"

"It's something I don't understand. I don't feel comfortable asking and I've even told myself that it's none of my business. But, as president of the society, I've come to the conclusion that if you're not going to tell us, then it's my obligation to ask."

"What are you trying to say?" Tamara asked sounding confused by Tom's rambling.

"What business do you have with Arthur Flemming?" he blurted.

There was a moment of silence before she asked, "Who?" Tamara felt her throat tighten. She knew her reply sounded immature. Feigning ignorance would just force Tom to become more direct. She shouldn't play this game with her good friend. She wished she could take back her "who."

"Tamara, I saw you with Flemming on the morning of the auction."

"It's not what you think, Tom."

"What is it, then?"

"Okay, let me start over. Yes I was with Arthur Flemming. I've met with him several times and I think he can help us."

Now it was Tom's turn to take pause. "Interesting," he finally said. "So you think that one of the Midwest's largest developers, ergo one of our biggest enemies, can be of help to us? I can't imagine what type of help you mean but I'm listening."

"I can't tell you right now."

"Tamara, don't do this to me."

"No, it's just that Robert is still here. He's in the bathroom getting ready to leave. I've already told him that I have too much business to take care of today and that I need to be alone. Once he's gone I can come over to see you and explain everything."

"Don't go anywhere. I'll be at your place in thirty minutes."

Tom turned around and began swiftly retracing his steps back to the house. He was just as curious as he had been before, but now he was more settled knowing that he would soon learn the answer to what puzzled him. He made it back to the house and into the kitchen where he saw Marina standing, smiling at him with Colleen at her side. Seeing them reminded him that he had forgotten all about the recital.

"Sweetheart," Tom said gazing at his daughter. "I have some urgent business to attend to and I'm so sorry but I won't be able to come to your voice recital."

Colleen's eyes were moist and Tom saw her lower lip curl and quiver ever so slightly. "Maybe Mom can record it for us," he suggested, turning to Marina. His wife's face didn't share the disappointment of her daughter's but, rather, conveyed a genuine look of concern.

# Chapter 9

As the door swung open his attention fixed on her eyes shining like emeralds, as he had never noticed before. He studied them, saying nothing, searching for answers.

"Don't look at me like that, Tom. You make me feel like a school girl who's disappointed her best friend."

"Have you?"

"Come on, Tom. How long have we known each other? Aren't you going to listen to my story before jumping to conclusions? Anyway, don't just stand there in the doorway. Come in."

"I suppose you're right," Tom said as he entered her town home. "Forgive me though if I've become alarmed after seeing my most trusted ally, the council's stabilizing influence, cavorting with the enemy."

"Cavorting?"

"Perhaps I used the wrong word. Considering you chose not to talk about it, your meeting would likely be categorized with the clandestine variety."

"Okay, enough. Let me tell you about it now."

Tamara sighed before beginning her story. "You know, though, your reaction is just the reason I was hesitant to involve any of you with this. You, Tom, of everyone, were the one I thought would be most understanding. If you won't even listen, I can't imagine anyone else will."

"Point taken and I apologize. But are you saying you haven't even spoken to Robert about this?"

"God, no. He wouldn't understand. After I'm through explaining things to you I was hoping that maybe you could speak with him."

"Me? He's your boyfriend."

"Sometimes I wish I'd never let things get this serious between

Robert and me. Don't get me wrong. He's a great guy, but I don't think we're meant for each other in that way. He can be irrational at times."

"Like me?"

"You're hardly irrational, Tom. Anyway, you didn't come here to hear about Robert and me. Let me tell you about Arthur Flemming."

Tamara started by informing Sanders that Flemming got his start in the development business by working for her parents. She mentioned that her parents still considered Flemming in high regard.

"Wow, you never told me Arthur Flemming was your parents' protégé."

"It wasn't something that I was particularly proud of. Besides, until two months ago, he wasn't someone that I ever expected to speak to again."

"So why are you talking to him now?"

"I felt that I owed it to him out of courtesy to my Mom and Dad. Then after listening to him, I discovered that he's not quite the evil caricature that we picture. He has a commonality with my parents in that he was successful, made some money—gobs more than my folks—and then had second thoughts on what it all meant. He's realized that chewing up the countryside in pursuit of the almighty buck isn't all what it's cracked up to be. Now he wants to help us."

"Arthur Flemming wants to help us?"

"Yes. Together, we might be able to prevent the forces that obliterated DeKalb County from destroying Ogle County too. For starters, he has a plan to slow down John Gardner. The LPS will insert a few wedges into Gardner's plans while, in the meantime, Arthur begins acquiring more and more land that can be saved from development."

"I understand that the eighty acres we purchased on Prairie Parkway might place a tiny wrench in Gardner's scheme, but you said 'wedges'. What other wedges might we have?"

"There's a large tract of land across the river to the southwest where an ancient Native American settlement once thrived. Apparently, county people were out there surveying and dug up some evidence that has yet to be made public. However, Arthur has a few contacts inside the county bureaucracy and he says that certain information is already beginning to leak. If this forces the finding to go public it's unlikely that the government will issue any development permits until there's been a full investigation. And guess what else. It just so happens that the land in question was the final property presented at last week's auction and of course you know who won that bid."

"Yes, of course. Go on."

"Well Arthur doesn't think his government sources are ready to squeal yet, but there's no reason we can't put a bug into a few ears ourselves and keep Gardner from moving too fast out there. So you see we do have more than one wedge. We've stymied Gardner's plans for Prairie Parkway and we can keep him preoccupied with the Native American land issue."

"This all sounds pretty sensational; however, Arthur Flemming and Pinnacle Development didn't build on the remains of Kane County and half of DeKalb County without having used a few people along the way. How do you know Flemming isn't using us now? He's ingenious; stir up the LPS to sidetrack GDC while his own Pinnacle Development makes a grand foray into Ogle County."

"Remember that I'm just as skeptical as you are when it comes to land sharks, Professor Sanders. I've considered what you suggest and even predicted that you would suspect much the same. Therefore, I thought that this afternoon would be a good time for you to meet with Flemming for yourself."

"You're kidding. Is he here?"

"No, but we can go over to his house to see him. I've already called to tell him to expect our visit."

"Uh, okay, let's go," Tom stuttered.

Without further discussion Tamara provided the address and they were in Sanders' vehicle heading toward Flemming's house. Tom stopped briefly on the entrance ramp to the expressway and declared "Exit thirty-one" into a small box before proceeding. After he steered into the right-hand lane his wheels were engaged by a tract that gradually shifted the vehicle over two lanes into the flow of traffic. They didn't notice when a larger, red vehicle carefully moved onto the same tract two slots behind to follow them. The roadway would automatically guide both vehicles to their intended exit ramp.

The motorists passed several large, relatively new housing plats as their vehicles were propelled over the expressway's surface. Each neighborhood in this area had the same basic plan. Perfectly straight streets, lined with three bedroom homes, were broken-up by rotaries on every second block. The rotaries were adorned with small green areas and every fourth block of these neighborhoods contained a larger park to accommodate organized sport and to provide a place where residents could stretch their legs. There were also more extravagant and imaginative developments in Ogle County, but this was one of several areas that Nathan Coulter referred to as his "functional neighborhoods."

Cornfields marked an abrupt end to the vast residential tracts on Ogle County's eastern edge. DeKalb wasn't designated "Agricultural" but the populace had voted to preserve a token to the county's heritage and maintained a narrow farming belt on the western boundary. The developers didn't complain too much because the preserve gave them a gimmick for selling expensive homes that overlooked the fields. They gave such communities names like "The Farms" or the "Fields of DeKalb."

"This area inspires me each morning when I pass on my way to preach about agrarian history at the University," Tom commented dryly as they rushed by the farmland.

"Really?"

"Maybe."

Soon they were back to rows of houses and Tom began quizzing Tamara again, "So how does Arthur Flemming go from making a fortune paving over land to suddenly wanting to help us preserve it?"

"The change wasn't necessarily that sudden. I checked out Pinnacle's more recent projects and noticed a pattern. Most of their activity has focused on large-scale commercial and residential renovation. They've started hardly any new developments in the last five years. Pinnacle seems to have become more interested in improving what's already been built rather than paving over open land."

"Or maybe, Flemming has run out of open land in the counties where he's normally operated and is just biding his time before expanding into Ogle County."

"Maybe, but that's why I wanted you to meet Arthur in person. You can ask him what he's up to for yourself."

The expressway continued catapulting them through various types of subdivisions, ones with one-acre lots, quarter-acre lots, small houses and large houses. There were business parks and commercial strips with every retail outlet imaginable. Out of DeKalb County and into Kane they drew closer to their exit and saw much of the same. Several miles later, Sanders' vehicle was gradually shifted over to the right until reaching the designated off ramp. As they coasted down from the expressway Tom shifted back to manual control and asked Tamara for more detailed directions to Flemming's house. The dark red vehicle was still lurking behind from a distance.

Tamara navigated Tom over a number of side streets until they reached the entrance to Flemming's neighborhood. It was a gated community and they were required to stop and speak to a guard before proceeding. "I guess this means Mr. Flemming doesn't like unannounced guests," Tom mumbled. "Pretty classy neighborhood though. They can afford to pay a real human for a security check."

Tamara ignored his comment and instructed him on what to say to gain access. Soon they were riding down curvy streets gawking at enormous luxury homes. The driver of the red vehicle didn't follow through the gate but instead came to a stop about a block away where a ghoulish grin crossed his face. He knew whom they were visiting so he was content to wait on the outside until they returned.

When Tom and Tamara reached the circular drive in front of Flemming's home a well-dressed man was waiting for them on a marbled walkway. The man quickly strode to the passenger's side as soon as their vehicle rolled to a stop. He opened the door for Tamara and bade a warm, yet formal greeting without introducing himself. Picturing the descriptions he'd received, Tom knew the man couldn't be Flemming.

"Mr. Flemming is waiting for you on the back terrace. I'll take you there," the man said.

Tom and Tamara were led into the house through an opulent foyer past two vast sitting rooms to a set of French doors that opened out to a large patio. The terrace stretched down to a kidney shaped pool that Arthur Flemming was aside under a canopied table. Flemming rose gracefully when he saw his guests coming. He swiftly walked to Tamara and gave her a hug and kiss on the cheek before extending his right hand to Tom.

"This must be the esteemed partner that you speak of Tamara. Welcome to my home, professor."

"Thank you. This is quite a place you have," Tom said feeling somewhat short in stature standing up next to Flemming's full height.

Tom studied the grounds as Flemming provided a brief history of how he came to build the home. Sanders' gaze wandered to a sandy beachfront abutting a good-sized lake that was undoubtedly the centerpiece of the gated community, planned and constructed by Pinnacle Development no doubt. The large estates visible across the water were each unique in character but none as lavish as Flemming's. Sensing he was missing the discussion describing what he saw, Tom turned his attention back to Flemming who was continuing his account now directed exclusively toward Tamara.

"I'm sorry for going on so before even offering you a drink."

Tom and Tamara's escort to the terrace, who had been waiting unassumingly just several steps away, took his bosses' cue and hurried to their sides. "We have a fine, crisp Pinot Grigio if you'd like. It seems perfect for this time of day at this time of year."

"That sounds good, Donald," Flemming answered decisively for his guests. "I think you'll like it, Tamara," he added.

Then, Flemming addressed Sanders again. "So, Tamara tells me that you're a professor concentrating in agricultural history. You look rather athletic and not nearly eccentric enough to be a professor."

"I guess I should take that as a compliment."

"You should, but I didn't mean it to sound like I had anything against professors or anything against agricultural history. As a matter of fact I've grown more fond of agriculture, rural life if you will, and open spaces over the years."

"Well there aren't a whole lot of farms left in this area and not all people equate agriculture with open space," Sanders couldn't help himself from responding but he did so in a strictly factual manner withholding passion from his argument. Tom was intent on remaining cool in order to carefully measure his nemesis allegedly turned ally. He couldn't afford to allow emotion to cloud his judgment.

"Indeed, professor; however, what's left is worth keeping and maybe not just for the sake of people here but also for the effects it has on other parts of the country."

Tom gently grasped his chin between his thumb and forefinger and was trying to grasp what Flemming meant when Donald reappeared with a tray carrying a bottle of wine and three glasses.

"I can understand that as a member of a radical group like the LPS that you're probably skeptical of a man like me," Flemming resumed as Donald filled the wine glasses.

"I suppose," Sanders responded softly.

Tom glanced toward Tamara as if he had been caught off guard. He was surprised that Tamara's newfound friend, if that's what Flemming was, spoke so openly. Theirs still needed to be a secretive society and Tom didn't feel comfortable with outsiders bringing up the society's name in conversation. However, Tamara's expression displayed no surprise on her part and suddenly Tom felt empowered as if Flemming's directness had broken down his need for caution.

"Okay, let me speak frankly," Sanders said more forcefully. Then, glimpsing at the pool and then back to Flemming's palatial residence over his shoulder he stated, "I am skeptical. A man doesn't amass a fortune in real estate development and then decide that what he's done is all wrong."

"Have I led you to believe that I think what I've accomplished is all wrong, professor?"

"Arthur, can you please call him Tom," Tamara finally interjected.

"Sure, if it's all right with him."

"Oh I suppose," Tom responded facetiously to elicit a chuckle from all three.

"Believe it or not, Tom, the economics of real estate development aren't what they used to be. Being a history professor perhaps you can appreciate what I'm saying. Oops, I'm sorry, Tamara, there I go using that professor word again."

"Go on, Arthur."

"Well, I'm sure you've studied Ronald Reagan and might be familiar with his twentieth century philosophy on supply side economics. The supply side was his barometer of economic health more so than demand. Lately I'm beginning to believe he was on to something. You see—there's still a huge demand for new homes because it seems that nobody wants to move into a place where somebody else has already lived. The problem is that we're running out of land upon which to build these new homes. The demand has killed the supply"

"Is that the real reason you're interested in Ogle County, because you're looking for more supply?" Tom asked holding no punches.

"There goes your skepticism again. Can you let him finish first?" Tamara scolded.

"That's okay, Tamara. Like I said, I can understand his doubts."

"You may have taken some liberties in your analysis of Reaganomics; however, I agree with most of the points you're making. It seems that no one wants to fix our old problems. The answer is always, let's just build a new one."

"Yes and that's why Pinnacle has changed our focus in recent years. There were some perfectly good neighborhoods built twenty, fifty and, sometimes, a hundred years ago, but they've had some wear and tear and no one wants to live there anymore. 'Build me a new home', they say. 'Gladly', the developer replies. 'There's money in it for me.' 'Gladly,' says the politician. 'There's money in it for me too."

"So you really think the politicians are in on it too?" Tamara asked rolling her eyes.

"Don't get me started," Flemming replied demonstratively. "Sure developers are greedy sons of guns, but it's the pols who violate public trust. Put enough money in their pocket and any development is gonna go through. I'll admit that I've paid them myself. They'll tell you that they're doing it for the community, but they don't really give a damn about that. They'll say it'll decrease taxes. But have you ever seen taxes go down after a development goes in? Of course not, the only thing you'll see go down is public service."

"You're starting to sound like one of those LPS radicals," Tom declared.

"Forgive me, I've digressed. My point is that we should be doing more redevelopment rather than new development. We've tried to recycle everything else in this country so why not refurbish our older neighborhoods?"

"Perhaps, for reasons not all that clear to themselves, our ancestors had things right," Tamara threw in. "They developed great cities for the benefit of the multitudes yet left the countryside to be the countryside. Now it's as if we live in a never-ending suburbia. It's hard to determine where the city begins or ends. That can't bode well for our long-term, collective psyche. At least, that's what some professor told me once," she finished, winking at Tom.

"We need to draw a line somewhere," Flemming confirmed.

"Somewhere like Ogle County?" Tom asked.

"Why not? There's still a bit of rural life that can be saved there."

"We'd be grateful for all the support we can get, but sometimes I think that it's already too late. I doubt we can garner much national support because it'd be difficult to argue that the country's dependent on Ogle's agricultural output."

"Yes, but the more we give in here the easier it is for them to take away open space somewhere else. It's the ripple effect. When buildings are constructed on top of farm fields, wheat fields have to be re-planted where grazing land stood pushing cattle into our national forests in search of fodder."

Maybe he is with us, Tom considered as he reflected on Flemming's comments.

"But explain to Tom what you think we can do in Ogle County," Tamara requested.

Flemming went on to detail much of what Tamara had already told Sanders. "We can delay GDC's development of the property across the river with the Native American find," he reiterated. "In the meantime, we can start to buy and hold more land."

"Don't get me wrong, because I think your plan has merit, but I doubt that even you have pockets deep enough to buy up all of Ogle County. The only long-term solution will be one that facilitates political reform."

"I know that's what the LPS is working for, but do you really have the network and credibility necessary to dig up enough controversy on Coulter's regime to bring about any change?"

Sanders just shrugged. He didn't like to think that their plans were known outside the council, but he couldn't deny that Flemming was probably right. Their chances of affecting political change were extremely dubious.

Tamara filled in for Tom's silence. "So Arthur, are you saying we're wasting our time by seeking reform?"

"No, not at all. I completely agree that political change is needed; however, I don't think you know Nathan Coulter like I know him. Buying a couple of properties and digging up a little dirt isn't going to phase Coulter. You're going to have to accumulate a lot more than that and take a few risks to get Coulter out into the open."

Tom Sanders couldn't help to notice the way Flemming spoke of Coulter. He knew that the Clerk was the most powerful official in Ogle County, but Flemming seemed to insinuate that Nathan Coulter was *"the"* government of the county. In any event, Sanders sensed that Flemming knew a whole lot more about the inner workings of the county's administration than the LPS did.

"So what do you suggest?"

"Doing exactly as we've discussed. We'll go about buying properties and eventually Coulter will step outside to see what we're up to. That's when he'll expose the skeletons lurking in his closet and then, just maybe, we'll have a chance to influence political change."

Tom looked down at his watch realizing his daughter's recital was long past over. "This is all very interesting, Arthur. I believe our alliance could have some real benefits. But let's resume our discussion later because, as for now, I really need to be going."

"I'd hoped that you'd both be able to stay for dinner."

"Your hospitality is appreciated, but I must be getting home."

"That's too bad, but how 'bout you Tamara? I can give you a ride home after dinner."

"Oh, it's way too far for you to have to drive me all the way home and then come all the way back."

"It's no bother and, besides, it'll give me a chance to run a few errands on my way home."

Tamara glanced nervously toward Tom before responding. "Yes, I suppose I could stay."

The spy who'd been patiently waiting for the LPS council members to return was confused when he saw Tom Sanders' vehicle exit from the gated community. There was no passenger. Should he follow the professor or wait to see if another vehicle came along?

# Chapter 10

Robert Sonnvoldt was tending the small flower garden in the front of his home when a limousine stopped at the curb. The limo was an unusual sight in his neighborhood where residents normally darted about in much smaller electric transports. Robert watched curiously as a well dressed, middle-aged black woman emerged from the passenger side. Must be someone looking for directions, he thought as the woman approached. No, I've seen her somewhere before, he reconsidered as she drew closer.

"Hello, Mr. Sonnvoldt. My name is Julie Dubose," she said offering her hand.

"Hello, Ma'am."

"This is quite a lovely garden you have here, Mr. Sonnvoldt."

"Thank you."

As Dubose scanned back and forth admiring the flowers the limo's driver slowly walked up and came to a stop several feet behind where she stood. He was a stocky man with a pale, ruddy complexion and seemingly uncomfortable in the business suit he wore. The unexpected visitors made an incongruent looking couple.

"How is it that you know me—Ms. Dubose I think you said it was?" Robert asked before realizing it was at the auction where he had seen the woman.

"Yes, Dubose is correct; however, you can call me Julie. Here's my card. I'm the Communications Director for Gardner Development Company and we met last week at the auction."

"We did?"

"Well, forgive me. We didn't actually introduce ourselves; however, after you made your purchases we spent a little time on our own to learn a bit about you. Gardner Development is always interested in the people who buy property in Ogle County."

"I think you said purchases as in plural. I only bought one property. That's all I could afford."

"Yes, of course," Dubose responded. By now, however, she knew that she was dealing with more than only Sonnvoldt and his relationship with Tamara Hopkins. Cristin Anelli persisted with her homework and had pieced together information connecting Robert, Tamara, as well as Thomas Sanders, to important positions within the LPS. Nevertheless, John Gardner remained content with his plan to exploit the Sonnvoldt-Hopkins romantic link. "It could be a divisive force within their organization," he maintained.

The man behind Julie Dubose had remained mum staring blankly at Robert all the while.

"Julie, aren't you going to introduce your friend?"

"This is Lucas," she said without acknowledging the oddity of his lurking about without participating in the conversation.

Lucas stepped up and extended his arm forward. He shook Robert's hand with a vise-like grip.

"Are you with GDC, too?"

"Yes," Lucas nodded.

"Mr. Sonnvoldt," Dubose continued as Lucas returned to his original position and folded his arms. "As to the purpose of my call, I misunderstood how much my boss wanted to acquire the property that you happened to purchase. I should have bid higher when we were at the auction. It's too late to change that now. However, there's no reason GDC can't purchase the property directly from you. I'm here to make you an offer."

"I'm a little puzzled," Robert said. "Is Lucas your boss?"

"No, I was referring to Mr. Gardner."

"I see. I appreciate the offer you'd like to make but as you may recall from the auction, that property is an old family farmstead. I'm not at all interested in selling it."

"We think that it was very nice that you were able to retain the farm for the family, too, so we'd hoped that you would keep it. It's the land that Tamara Hopkins won at the auction that John Gardner wants to buy."

Robert cleared his throat. "Tamara Hopkins? Why are you here to see me then?"

"We thought that you could help us explain the benefits of the deal to Ms. Hopkins."

"How would I help? I don't even know who you're talking about."

"Come now, Mr. Sonnvoldt. I told you we like to learn something about the people who buy property in this county. Certainly you must suspect that we know that Ms. Hopkins is your girlfriend."

"I don't see how it would be any of your business if she was," Sonnvoldt replied. He was noticeably agitated.

"I'm sorry if I offended you."

"That's okay. There probably isn't a whole lot more for us to talk about anyway so why don't you and your partner hop back into your shiny limousine and head back to your office."

"Look, Mr. Sonnvoldt, you're right. It's none of our business to know whether you even have a girlfriend. But, the fact is, we came to know that you have a relationship with Ms. Hopkins so let's try to put that intrusion behind us. We're not here to irritate you. We just think that we have a proposal that can benefit all parties involved."

"I'm not Tamara Hopkins' negotiator."

"Of course not. But maybe you'll be more understanding of our offer."

"Excuse me if I've led you to believe that I'm trying to be understanding."

"Please, Mr. Sonnvoldt," Dubose pleaded politely. "I'm prepared to offer you a lot of money."

"Shouldn't you be offering it to Ms. Hopkins?"

"This was Ms. Hopkins first purchase. She may be emotionally attached to the idea of holding on to the property. You can explain to her that we're offering much more for the land than it is even worth. She'll be able to use the proceeds to buy a bigger property. She can buy something out close to where your farm is. Wouldn't it be nice if you two could accumulate some land out there?"

Ms. Dubose's pleasant tone and helpful suggestions weren't making Robert feel any more comfortable. The henchman who continued to stare disturbingly from over the woman's shoulder was a big contributor to his unease and Sonnvoldt just wanted to say something to make his uninvited guests leave as soon as possible. "Fine," he declared. "Write down your best offer. If it looks like it's worth my time, maybe I'll show it to her."

Julie Dubose smiled. "It's already drawn up. I have a copy waiting on the front seat. Let me get it for you."

GDC's communications officer strolled to the limo, opened the passenger door and retrieved a small document. This number should show him the light she thought confidently while returning to Sonnvoldt's yard. However, as she neared the two men she had left alone only momentarily, her face instantly turned to a grimace when she overheard that unpleasantly familiar, raspy voice. "Julie didn't explain the risks Miss Hopkins could avoid if she sells that property."

"What do you mean, the risks?" Robert asked.

"Well, it'd be risky owning land where Mr. Gardner wants to build. Probably be a lot safer over by your farm. You understand."

"Lucas!" Julie Dubose interrupted firmly. "We're almost finished so why don't you go wait in the vehicle."

"Sure, no problem. Pleasure meeting you, Mr. Sonnvoldt," Lucas said reaching to shake Robert's hand again. The grip was even firmer than the first time they shook.

As the henchman made his way back to the limo Dubose handed Robert the document and said, "Please don't pay too much attention to Lucas. I'm sure he meant well by whatever he said but he's not supposed to be getting involved in business details. So please take a few moments to look over our offer sheet. I'll call you tomorrow evening to see what you think."

Sonnvoldt scanned the paper quickly as Dubose turned to leave. He was astonished by the amount he saw. These people truly were serious.

While the limousine was still rolling away from the curb Julie pursed her lips and asked sternly, "Why did you have to open your mouth, Lucas?"

"What da ya mean?"

"I mean bringing up the risks already!"

"He didn't seem cooperative as he should. I figured he could use something to think about."

As Lucas drove on Dubose turned away in disgust and stared out the window. "You could have waited until after I received their response to the offer sheet," she concluded before riding the rest of the way back to their home office in silence.

# Chapter 11

"What'd he say?" John Gardner asked impatiently almost before Julie Dubose had a chance to disconnect from her conversation with Robert Sonnvoldt.

"He's mulled over our offer but says he needs more time."

"More time? We've already given him a day!"

"I know, John. But he says that he's not used to doing business with people like us and he hasn't brought himself to discussing our proposal with Hopkins yet. He'd like for us to give him until the end of the week to make his decision."

"Maybe it's time to send in Lucas and his boys."

"No! Please don't send in those barbarians yet," Dubose pleaded. It's not going to kill us if we wait another week."

"Patience hasn't always been one of my strong suits, Julie. I didn't build Gardner Development Company to what it is today by waiting for things to happen."

"Yes, sir. But sometimes patience can be an asset and plus we have our public image to consider. We don't want people to think that we're bullies."

"Okay, we'll give this thing until the weekend. Keep in touch with him over the next few days, however, so that he doesn't forget about us. In the meantime, I'll see what else Cristin can find out about these LPS people."

Ten miles away, at her office, Tamara Hopkins was receiving a call from Tom Sanders.

"Still working late hours, ha Tam."

"We can't all have the same cushy summer hours that you professors enjoy."

"Well, some of us can't work all night. We have families at home to consider. By the way, what time did Arthur get you home last night?"

"I wasn't really watching the clock."

"Sounds like it must have been pretty late."

"You're not jealous are you, Tom?"

"No, I just worry about you."

"Thanks, big bro, but I can take care of myself."

"Good. Well, anyway, I've given our chat with Arthur a lot of thought. I think having someone with real estate expertise and financial clout on our side could give the LPS a boost. I'm game for seeing if we can work with him."

"Why not, what do we have to lose?"

"Our pride. But even if our alliance fails maybe we can learn something from him. I'll arrange a council meeting for tomorrow night to see if we can get consensus on this idea."

Tom was accelerating their schedule. The LPS council had already been set to meet the following Tuesday to continue strategizing on their primary objective: uncovering and publicly disclosing improper dealings between large developers and government officials. This was the only way the council believed they could garner public support for slowing the tide of building expansion that threatened to overwhelm the lands of Ogle County. Only when people grew disgusted with the corruption and greed involved in the land grant and building approval process would they care enough to ask more questions and hold the elected accountable. If the public only knew how much they ultimately sacrificed by allowing a relatively few benefactors to become wealthy by offering promises they never intended to fulfill. If they only knew, the public would jump in to help stop the devastation. Certainly that was what the LPS were counting on.

Surveillance of the events at and surrounding the auction had produced entertaining discussion material. However, Tom Sanders realized that the council was no closer to having hard evidence than they were before. The LPS just didn't have enough inside sources to reliably follow up on leads. Sanders still believed that their strategy focused on the right goal, but he wasn't certain whether they'd ever uncover the extent of corruption that actually existed and thus be capable of swaying public opinion.

The council's success with obtaining two properties was energizing and finally gave them control over something tangible. However, ultimately, their success threatened to divert them from their primary objective. Tom envisioned that the majority of next Tuesday's meeting would be devoted to talking about safeguarding their acquisitions. But realistically what could they do with only two properties?

Then, out of the blue, along comes Arthur Flemming offering to lend assistance. Tom wasn't keen to the idea at first, but after evaluating the Society's weaknesses he reconsidered. Flemming might shed light on back-room political dealings like they'd never seen before and if he chose to share his financial resources that would be another plus. Besides, Flemming's involvement wouldn't alter the council's objectives, he'd merely help reshape their tactics and, hopefully, for the better.

Tamara had tried to downplay her exuberance over Tom's decision to work with Flemming. As a result, she was too pre-occupied to allow his last comment to sink in at first. "Hold on," she finally objected. "Did you say you wanted to talk to the council about Arthur's proposal tomorrow night? Do you really think they're ready to consider a partnership with Arthur Flemming?"

"Maybe not, but we'll never know without discussing it."

"Arthur told me that he'd like to acquire two more properties before laying the plan out for the full council. He thinks it'll be easier to explain the concept once we have more land and can show our strength."

"We can't do that to our partners, Tamara!" Sanders exclaimed. "We can't, in good conscience, unveil a major plan months after it's already been put in motion. It's unfortunate that we've been forced into keeping our activities secret from the government; however, we won't keep secrets from our own council members. We can lead them, we can persuade them, but we can't keep them in the dark. In the end, if they decide to reject our recommendation then so be it. We'll move forward and consider other options."

"Yeah that's what I told Arthur you'd say," Tamara responded sheepishly.

"I'm serious, the LPS has to be united on this matter," Tom reemphasized. He knew that if the council were to be united they would have to do so quickly. Andy, Jason or, particularly, Robert might lose their trust in Tamara if they thought she'd been formulating plans on her own for too long and was somehow in cahoots with Flemming. Tamara's perspective and tempering influence were too vital to the group for Tom to allow that to happen.

"You're right. Let's talk to the council right away."

"Tomorrow night."

"Tomorrow night," she agreed.

Robert Sonnvoldt had no problem honoring Tom's request to get together on short notice. He was still charged up about his encounter with GDC and was bristling to unveil his own tantalizing tidbits. Andy Cemanski and Jason McAlpin were also more than accommodating. They were both eager to press forward with action plans discussed at the last meeting. Cemanski ever ready, ever vigilant, was first to arrive that evening.

"We've got to stop meeting like this," Andy declared when Tom opened the door. "I mean at your home that is. You may be starting to draw attention here."

"I know, but I didn't have time to think of any alternatives."

"I just hope Tamara and Robert aren't foolish enough to carpool again."

"They're not likely to after the tongue lashing you gave them last time," Tom retorted sarcastically.

Andy's concern was soon alleviated when Tamara drove up, alone. When everyone else had arrived, Sanders wasted no time in calling the meeting to order. "I know we were going to wait another week; however, there has been a development that could alter our agenda. Someone who thinks that he can lend support to our cause has approached us and I thought it best to get this matter out on the table as soon as possible."

"You mean we've finally found a politician willing to take the high road?" Andy Cemanski smirked.

"Not exactly."

"Who then?"

"Arthur Flemming, founder and CEO of Pinnacle Development Company."

"That's pretty good, Tom. What other material do you got?" Jason McAlpin quipped.

"I'm serious, he thinks we can work together."

"No shit?" Andy muttered with dropped jaw. "You don't really believe him?" he quickly added while raising his voice.

"My first reaction was similar to yours, Andy. But after talking to him he sounds sincere."

"What type of assistance is he proposing?" Jason asked.

"He has information that if used properly could prevent GDC from developing the large parcel that they picked up in the southwest. At the same time, in concert with us, he believes we can slowly make purchases to keep other properties from being developed as well. Eventually, if we accumulate enough land we just might draw the politicians out for a look, which will leave them vulnerable and allow us to expose their misdeeds."

"How do we know we can trust him?"

"We can't!" Andy barked.

"Yeah, what if he's just using us as Pinnacle's entrée to Ogle County? Who's to say he doesn't buy up a whole lot of property and then start building on it himself?"

"Possible," Tom had to admit. "But if that happened, are we any worse off than if GDC or any of those other sharks bought the property?"

"Yeah but the more maggots there are, the faster the carcass is likely to be devoured," Andy responded cynically.

"How did Flemming find you anyway, Tom?" Robert asked.

"He didn't."

"You went to him?"

"No, he found Tamara."

Robert jerked his head around toward Tamara; his eyes questioning in astonishment. Tamara had feared just this moment, but she resolved herself to respond. "Mr. Flemming actually worked for my parents years ago. I never maintained contact with him but he knew who I was, of course, and somehow he figured out my association with the LPS. So he called me several weeks prior to the auction. I didn't bother to tell anyone because I didn't take him seriously at first. But the more I listened the more his story seemed to have merit. That's when I asked Tom to talk with him, so he could help me decide whether Flemming's suggestion was worth the council's consideration."

"You never once thought you should tell me about this?" Robert asked demandingly.

Tamara pursed her lips as she glanced at Robert sensing that now was not the time to explain her thoughts and emotions to him. She turned toward Tom, seeking reassurance, before continuing to speak. "Tom helped clarify matters. Arthur Flemming is extremely wealthy and has the wherewithal to acquire more property than we will ever have on our own. He also has multitudes of contacts in not only the real estate business but also in the government. He could be a tremendous asset to our cause. We could be wasting a great opportunity if we don't explore the potential of this partnership."

An awkward silence permeated the room when Tamara finished. Robert gazed at the walls looking at nothing in particular. Tamara felt Andy's stare and then Jason's transfixed upon her, studying her, wondering. She grew more uncomfortable as each second passed. They'd never looked at her like this before, now accusingly, as if her position of honor and esteem had been unceremoniously rescinded.

Tom searched for the right words but he couldn't think of what to say to break the impasse. Finally, Robert's voice breached the silence.

"I have another alternative."

The comment came unexpectedly and didn't register with the group. "Do you want to hear about it?" he coaxed.

"Go on," Tom dryly encouraged.

"I was approached by GDC the other day and received another offer."

"Jesus!" Andy exclaimed. "What have we been doing, passing out business cards to every developer in the land?"

"I guess our society isn't so secret anymore," Jason added.

"I've heard enough," Andy continued. "Let's just invite all the developers over and have one big love-fest."

"Let's settle down," Tom implored. "We need to hear what type of offer Robert received. Let him speak."

"Fine. Go ahead, Robert. This should be interesting."

Robert looked over his partners nervously. He was still anxious to relay his encounter with John Gardner's bidding agent but he hadn't anticipated their skepticism. Perhaps he'd underestimated Andy's animosity toward GDC. But certainly, Robert had never expected to hear that while he was mulling over Julie Dubose's offer, his girlfriend was simultaneously working a deal with another developer. Then he spoke. "They came to my house to tell me they'd like to buy the property that Tamara won at the auction. They made a substantial offer and I've given it a lot of thought. I'm thinking that it wouldn't be a bad idea to accept it."

"Wow, Robert. I'm all ears. Tell us why it wouldn't be a bad idea to do business with GDC," Andy requested mockingly.

"Well, there's more to it. If we sell Tamara's property on Prairie Parkway, they'll help us get some land in the northwest, out by my property. I was thinking that if we can obtain enough land in that area we'll be able to establish a power-base."

"Have we all gone mad?"

"Come on, Andy, think about it. What are we going to accomplish by purchasing a few acres here and there, scattered all over the county. We need a stronghold."

Through the initial banter over Robert's revelation Tamara remained mute, still feeling the effects of the icy response to her own disclosure. But suddenly she rose up, transforming from the accused to the accuser. "GDC approached you to buy my property?" she questioned. "Shouldn't you have told me about this immediately?"

Robert returned her glare. "As if you've were forthcoming about your trysts with the rich playboy."

"I think I'm capable of understanding the facts. I was afraid that you weren't and it seems that I was correct," Tamara snipped.

Tom felt all semblance of order slipping away. There had been disagreements at previous council meetings, but there had always been a mutual trust and each one understood that they were working toward the same goal. But now the group was imploding before his eyes?

"Hold on," he demanded firmly without raising his voice. "First of all, let's dismiss this concept of *"his"* property and *"her"* property. Remember that society funds were used to purchase those properties."

Tamara cheeks flushed as Tom spoke. "I'm sorry, I didn't really mean to imply that it was my property."

"Okay," Tom nodded. "Secondly, I don't like the idea of rubbing elbows with the developer's either. But let's face it, eventually this was bound to happen and we're going to have to get on the radar screen to make any real impact anyway."

"You may be right," Andy interjected but in a calmer tone than before, "but if we become too big of a blip before we have the ammo to fight back the government's gonna cut us off at the knees again."

"Guys, I hate to tell you this but they don't use radar screens anymore. They just dial right into your living room. Right now they can probably tell you what color underwear my wife's wearing."

Tom chuckled at Jason's retort but he realized that their conversation had reached diminishing returns. Even though the group had settled down he sensed they were still on separate pages. Tamara was acting in a manner he'd never seen before, somewhat mysterious lately and now a little adolescent. Robert was sulking. Andy was his usual self but his cynicism toward anyone labeled developer would make coming to terms with Arthur Flemming difficult. "Okay gang," Tom concluded, "I don't think we're going to resolve anything tonight. So everyone go home, get some rest and digest these new events. I'll call everyone tomorrow to see if we can concur on what direction to take."

"That's fine," Andy replied. "I need to get home anyway. My grandkids are coming to town so I need to get some sleep and be ready to spoil them rotten tomorrow." Everyone else agreed to adjourn as well and after latching the door behind the last of them, Tom closed his eyes and raised one hand to his forehead. Standing there grimacing, he slowly ran his fingers through his hair and over the top of his head until they clasped the back of his neck. He was beginning to comprehend the challenges that would arise throughout the course of his leadership mission. Their increasing clarity made them all the more daunting.

# Chapter 12

After lobbying his fellow council members through most of the morning, Tom called Tamara with welcome news. "I think we're back on track. Andy and Jason agreed to give our alliance with Flemming a try."

"After last night I sure didn't expect to hear that."

"Yeah, how did Andy put it?—'GDC is the devil no doubt and Flemming probably is, too, but as long as Arthur stays decent enough to keep a lid over his horns I guess we can give him a chance.' Of course Andy let me know that he'd be 'watching Flemming like a hawk.'"

"Yup, that sounds like Andy. You didn't mention Robert, though. Has he agreed with this?"

"Well, it probably helped that I called him after Andy and Jason and was able to tell him that they were already on board. But—did Robert agree with the plan? That might be an overstatement. Let's just say he acquiesced."

"I'm amazed you even got that far."

"Yeah, he was pretty intent on accumulating more land in the northwest and I could tell he's still bothered about your association with Arthur."

"My association? I thought we were in this together, Tom."

Tom smiled. "We are. Anyway, I told him that I respected his idea and agreed that it would be nice to be able to establish an enclave somewhere but the timing just isn't right. He, too, realizes that our resources are limited and we could have only so much impact by trying to accumulate property in one area, particularly on our own. Our primary objective currently focuses on gathering support to foster a more broad-based movement that helps preserve open space throughout the county. I think

Robert understands the possibilities of what might be accomplished by building stronger alliances, but I think you've bruised his ego. You may have to stroke him a little bit."

Tamara wrinkled her nose as she considered Tom's last comment. Then she responded, "I'm not sure I'm capable of that right now because I'm feeling rather humbled myself. It's one thing to stir up controversial discussion but I think I came close to breaking up the council by not properly communicating the facts and allowing them to jump to conclusions. I could have ruined everything for the society if it weren't for you bailing me out and picking up the pieces."

"That's what I'm here for."

"Seriously, Tom. I let my emotions and ego come before the interests of the society."

"Emotions are a necessary ingredient for our success. We can't just draw up a plan and expect it to work. Does a chef become great by picking up a recipe and following along step by step? No, they need to have passion and have a sense for when to improvise."

"Sure, but I'm supposed to be a sophisticated businesswoman. Last night I was acting like a schoolgirl. I was a lot more harm than help to the council."

"Nonsense, you've been of great help to the council. You've presented us with a tremendous opportunity. We wouldn't be discussing a partnership with Arthur Flemming and the possibilities that might bring if it weren't for you. You're an engaging, attractive woman. Do you think Arthur would have asked me out for lunch?"

"Great, now you're implying that my feminine attributes are my only worth to this organization and that Arthur's using the LPS to get in bed with me."

Tom blushed. "Sorry, perhaps what I said didn't come out right. I was just trying to say that we need you and you needn't hide your feelings. Wisdom and emotion are not mutually exclusive. Besides, there'll be plenty of chances for you to bail me out. Like right now, you can help me get my foot out of my mouth."

"I'll forgive you, professor, but only if you'll tolerate my schoolgirl behavior every once in a while."

"Agreed."

"So do you really think working with Arthur is the right thing to do?"

"Time will tell. But, in the meantime, let's get this rolling before anyone changes his mind. I've a few appointments to keep and then I'll stop by your office so that we call Arthur together."

Flemming sounded elated when he heard from them. "That's great news! I can't wait to get started. I've already come up with a few more ideas."

"Let's not allow our emotions to run too far ahead of ourselves, Arthur." Tamara recommended while directing a knowing smile toward Tom. "I think you should meet the other members of our council first."

"Of course."

"Maybe it wouldn't be wise for us to gather in person just yet, but we can arrange for a conference call. That'll give our partners the opportunity to hear your voice and listen to your ideas first-hand."

"Okay, set it up."

They ended their conversation cordially and with guarded enthusiasm but before Flemming mentioned that he'd already put certain plans in action and had arranged a meeting with Nathan Coulter. Later that night, Flemming entered the foyer of a small, but upscale, restaurant in DeKalb County midway between his home and Coulter's political bastion. The hostess instantly welcomed him and said, "Mr. Coulter is waiting at his table, please follow me." *I shouldn't be surprised that he has everything prepared,* Flemming thought as he strolled past several tables.

The diminutive politician stood to greet the tall businessman when he reached the corner table in the back of the restaurant. "I hope you found you're way okay. A good friend of mine owns this place. The food is outstanding and I don't think we'll have to worry about too many people seeing us here together."

"Do I embarrass you, Nathan?" Flemming asked sarcastically.

"You never lose your wit do you, Arthur? The answer is no, it's just that back in my county any time I meet with one of your type someone notices and wants to know where the next big project is going to be."

The two men briefly exchanged small talk before Coulter got to business. "I know that you requested this meeting but before you start let me first congratulate you on your Ogle County land purchase. You haven't been active in my county for sometime, so don't think your acquisition didn't create a stir. Gardner was more than a little upset. He thinks I should have warned him that you were jumping back in. No problem though, a little competition is good for the county. But you'll have to give me some detail on your intentions. I need to assure that we keep an orderly flow to these things."

"Are you worried about what John Gardner thinks?"

"I didn't say that. Like I did say, we just like to keep an orderly flow to things in Ogle County."

Such a typical Nathan Coulter speech, Flemming thought. He's the master at making his point so succinctly with the use of such vague terminology. "I think I understand," he responded. "That's why I asked to see you. It's no skin off of my nose but I've heard rumor that the property Gardner purchased in the southwest part of the county is home to an ancient Indian burial ground."

"I didn't know that you were an archaeologist, Arthur."

"Certainly you've heard the rumors?"

"I'm sure Indians roamed that area at one time but no, I haven't heard any rumors about burial grounds. No one's dug up any artifacts and placed them on my desk." Since they'd greeted one another Nathan Coulter maintained a smile, so ingenuous it seemed as if it must have been painted on by one of his aides, but now one eye became barely a slit. What could be seen of his lips began slowly curling downward. "What are you trying to get at, Arthur?"

Flemming was worried that he'd presented the issue too early in their conversation but now he was in such position where he had to press forward. "I just know how much you like to keep an orderly flow and I was worried that the waters could get choppy if the public found out that you issued a development permit to GDC that allowed them to build right over the top of an Indian burial ground."

"Look," Coulter shot back in warning. "I'm not sure what you're up to but you'd better come clean with me. We've seen you with the Hopkins woman. She's a looker so I can't fault you for that but if it means you're getting involved with the LPS you'd better stop right now."

The businessman was caught off guard by the powerful politician's rapid counterattack but able to recover by feigning resentment. "What would a guy like me have to do with the LPS?"

"I have no idea but we've found out that the Hopkins woman is high up in their organization."

"It's a coincidence. I worked with Tamara Hopkins many years ago and happened to run into her. After that I've been trying to rekindle our connection. We're both single, you know. However, we haven't got around to comparing our political ideologies yet."

"When you come to see me and start talking about Indian burial grounds after you've been sleeping with the LPS, I don't like it. The LPS is a non-starter with me. Years ago, they caused me a lot of trouble and I spent too much time and effort getting them put in the place where they're at today. The LPS is inconsequential in my county today and

I better never find out that someone has ideas about resurrecting them. Is that clear!"

"I can assure you, Nathan, that I have no interest in the LPS."

"My blood pressure rises every time I see Andy Cemanski. That son of a bitch almost cost me my first election. I'd put him in jail again if I didn't think that they'd rally around him to gather sympathy for their cause."

"I didn't come here to rile you, Nathan. Let me tell you what this is really all about. I don't give a damn about the Indian burial grounds. But if I can use them to slow down Gardner they might buy me enough time so that I can gain a foothold in Ogle County. If he has to avoid the press and work through your office to get the approvals needed to start his project, he'll be too pre-occupied to worry about me."

"Are you asking me to waste my time with this mess?"

"No, I'm really trying to work with you on this. You know, maintain an orderly flow. If the public found out a project got rammed through on that land I think you'd end up wasting a whole lot more of your time on damage control than you'll ever spend with me or John Gardner."

"So how many people know about these burial grounds?"

"Nobody that's likely to go public," Flemming answered coldly. Inside, however, he winced. This was the dangerous part to the game. Surely, Coulter would do some checking. What was the chain of title on the property? Who surveyed the site and with whom were they connected? If Coulter found out exactly what Flemming knew and from whom he learned it, then he'd regain the upper hand. If this happened Coulter would have no reason to help him at the risk of alienating John Gardner.

"Let me see if there is anything I can do for you, Arthur," Coulter said as he picked up a menu seemingly able to instantly temper his agitated state. "In the meantime, let's eat. I'm getting hungry."

They finished dinner without raising the issue again. The opening discussion didn't go the way Arthur Flemming had planned but he was satisfied that he had recovered. Flemming remained resolved. One way or the other he was going to make an impact in Ogle County.

Flemming moved for the bill when it was presented. "Not this time, comrade," Coulter said as he pushed the reaching hand aside. Then, he added, "I hope you don't mind if I don't walk outside with you. I want to catch up with my friend and see how his restaurant business is going."

"I don't mind at all. It's late and I should be hurrying along anyway."

They shook hands and as Flemming turned to leave he heard Coulter clear his throat. "Oh, Arthur, just one more thing. If you really want to make a splash in Ogle County why haven't you considered using the old-fashioned way?"

"And what way would that be?"

"Cash," Coulter said while a thin-lipped smile crept across his face.

# Chapter 13

"Call him right away. Make it sound routine, but let him know there could be a delay before the development permit is granted," Coulter instructed. "I'd call myself but I don't want Gardner reading more into this than he has to."

Coulter had wasted no time following up on Flemming's disclosure about the Indian burial grounds. Apparently, Flemming hadn't been blowing smoke over dinner the night before. Several of Coulter's senior aides had heard the same rumor. However, it was one of those rumors where no one could quite place who they'd heard it from.

"Damn, that must mean every Tom, Dick and Harry knows about this." That's when Coulter ordered the call to Gardner. He didn't mind Flemming's foray into Ogle County. That was good for business. However, he didn't care to leave Gardner with the impression that he was withholding information to favor Arthur Flemming. That would be bad for business.

Not surprisingly, Coulter's scheme to make the matter seem routine wasn't working. He knew it wouldn't. Before long, his aide was informing him that Gardner wanted to see him as soon as possible.

"Tell him I've got twenty minutes at three thirty," Coulter sighed.

Gardner was prompt for the meeting just as Coulter expected and he got right to the point. "Is this some kind of joke, Nate? Bass tells me there's a bunch of old Indians buried on my property."

"We're not sure yet. If you'll pardon the pun, we need to dig into it a little further."

"Get a bigger shovel then, because I want to know what's going on."

"I understand why you'd be anxious, John. But I think we need to proceed cautiously on this matter. We don't want to stir up the public. That wouldn't be good for either one of us."

"You're right about that but, tell me, did you know anything about this before the auction?"

"I only found out about the damn thing this morning," Coulter stretched the truth not mentioning he'd had dinner with Flemming the previous evening. "I had Bass call you immediately. We don't know the magnitude of the problem but I wanted to alert you in case it causes some delay. I suspect that this is a minor issue and we'll find our way around it rather quickly."

"Maybe it is a minor issue but you know what, it's your issue! If the county let me buy tainted property, then you should refund my money."

The crafty politician shifted uncomfortably in his chair. He hadn't considered this point. Gardner presented a worthy argument. How could the county sell land without disclosing potentially important development restrictions? Land could be sold as is, but that condition had to be stated in advance. Coulter was embarrassed that he'd been caught off guard. He prided in his preparation, normally responding as if he were reading from a script.

"Did you hear what I said, Nate?"

"I heard you. You want me to buy back your land." Coulter's embarrassment quickly changed to annoyance bordering on outright anger. But he wouldn't allow himself to become angry just yet. No, that would be a sign of weakness and Nathan Coulter only displayed rage when it was necessary to emphasize his position. Besides, it wasn't John Gardner who had swelled his irritation.

"I'd like my money back but I'm not ready to give the land back yet. When will you tell me whether or not a permit is going to be issued?"

"I'm not sure but I'll let you know as soon as I have sufficient information to make a decision."

"Look, I mean it when I say I should get a refund. However, the problem is, that damn woman came out of nowhere to acquire a property that fits into one of my puzzles. I tell myself that it's okay because I'll just buy it back from her later. Then Flemming shows up and buys the other piece of my puzzle. What the hell is going on with that?"

"I don't know."

"Exactly, you don't know or at least you say you don't. So I can't afford to give away more property and more leverage. I pay a lot of money to people to come up with ideas and to look for opportunities. But unless I'm developing property and putting up buildings no one's paying me. So until I get the property back from the Hopkins woman or until you tell me what Flemming's up to I'm not giving back your cemetery."

"Be patient, John, you'll get your development permit. In the meantime, I can provide you with an interesting tidbit." The teaser was a manifestation of Coulter's anger toward Arthur Flemming for embroiling him in this most unpleasant situation. He was planting a seed to pit Gardner against Flemming and to get him off his back. Coulter wasn't about to risk the public's ire or have either one of the developers manipulate his office. He would, however, allow the business behemoths to wage battle amongst themselves.

Gardner took the bait and asked, "What kind of tidbit?"

"Did you know that Tamara Hopkins serves on the LPS council?" Coulter started before Gardner interrupted.

"I make it my business to know something about each and every person who purchases land in this county. So tell me something that I don't know."

"It seems that Arthur Flemming has a lustful eye directed at Ms. Hopkins."

Gardner furrowed his brow. "You're not saying that Flemming's become part of the LPS?"

"No, but I think he'd like Ms. Hopkins to think that he's on their side. It's funny how low some men will stoop in attempt to shag a woman."

Gardner's emotions may have been stirred and his mind raced but he didn't let on. "That is interesting, Nate," he responded. "But we're getting a little old to sit around gossiping about who's doing who. Unless I can figure out how to use information to my benefit it has no value to me."

"I'm sure you'll figure out how to use the information to your benefit soon enough. Why don't you call me next week? By that time, I'll have more news on the Indian burial grounds."

# Chapter 14

The shadows were disappearing into the late August evening air and Marina didn't notice the vehicle quietly slide past the side of the house. She was too busy talking to her husband on the direct link from his auto.

"I know, honey," Tom replied. "I'm later than I thought I'd be but I should be home in less than twenty minutes."

"You were aware that it was a surprise party?" Marina questioned sarcastically.

"Yes. We can still get there in time for dinner."

"You mean dessert."

"I'm sorry but I really needed to give my assistants feedback on the syllabus they're proposing. They need to be prepared for classes starting on Monday."

"Couldn't you have had them come in on Saturday instead?"

"It'd have been too late. They'll be using the weekend to make adjustments. Come on, you know I'd rather be with you," Tom pleaded sincerely.

"Okay, we'll be ready to leave as soon as you get home." Marina concluded as she felt a trace of remorse overcome her. I must have sounded catty, she thought. There's no reason to weigh him down with more concerns. She knew that Tom had been preoccupied with LPS activities and, at least from his point of view, he had been neglecting his course work and research. This bothered him terribly so the last thing he needed was to have his wife make him feel guilty about missing his aunt's surprise birthday party. There would be plenty of other guests to ring in another year for auntie dear.

While Marina was completing her conversation a sturdy man of average height was stepping out of the vehicle that had rolled to a stop behind the Sanders' residence. He immediately began surveying the grounds to the rear of the house. The sun was almost completely below the horizon now; individual trees were virtually indiscernible, as the orchard had become one dark mass. Good, he thought as he slid a mask over his head, there won't be any neighbors spying on me tonight. The man had been assured that the family would be out and the mask was only meant as a precaution in the event the home was equipped with a video monitoring system.

The man turned his attention to the house. There were more lights on than he had expected but the property seemed secluded enough. He didn't worry as he grabbed a laser knife from the front seat and proceeded to the back door that opened into a utility room that led on to the kitchen. The laser easily pierced the door lock and he was into the home in a matter of seconds.

Marina, meanwhile, walked toward the kitchen after disconnecting with her husband. Well if I'm going to miss the cocktail hour, she thought, I might as well pour myself a glass of wine to enjoy here before we leave. She walked in the kitchen opposite from where the intruder was entering through the utility room. She gasped in astonishment when she saw him. The man was just as startled. He hadn't anticipated finding anyone in the house.

"What are you doing here?" her voice rang out in a peculiar melody that mixed righteousness with apprehension.

The man replied simply by drawing a small pistol from his pocket. He looked her up and down deliberately and then asked gruffly through the mask, "Where's your husband?"

She hesitated, contemplating, before responding, "He's at the neighbor's. They're looking for a tool. They'll be right back."

Then from the staircase, Marina's daughter yelled out, "Mom, when is Dad going to be home from work?"

The intruder instantly detected Marina's lie and put a finger to his mouth, motioning her further into the kitchen with his pistol.

"Mom, I can't find my blue shoes."

The burglar slowly moved closer to the door from where Colleen's voice was coming. As he peeked around the corner trying to surmise the girl's exact location Marina quietly lifted a kitchen knife off a rack on the counter.

"Mom, where are you?" the voice came edging nearer the kitchen. As soon as Colleen came through the door the stranger wrapped the arm of his gun hand firmly around her waist and used his free hand to cover her mouth.

"Let her go!" Marina screamed.

The man shoved the girl away and she spun, stumbling toward her mother.

"Quiet, I said!"

"What do you want? We'll give you our money. Just please leave," Marina pleaded still frantic but using a somewhat mellower tone.

"There's more to it than that, Mrs. Sanders." His words were eerie. He obviously knew exactly whose house he was burglarizing. Who was he? A disgruntled legal client or perhaps someone she had contested in court?

"Tell us what you need and you can be on your way."

"That would be very accommodating of you, Mrs. Sanders. Why yes, maybe you can help. Tell me, where does the professor keep his society information? Oh, and after that, you can help me ransack the house."

"What society information?"

"No need to play coy, Mrs. Sanders. You see, my mission is very clear. Find some information: names, dates, plans and so forth. Then send a message by destroying a few personal articles."

"Why don't you let us leave so that you can finish your work uninterrupted?"

"I don't think that would be wise. You present an interesting twist to my mission. I was told that no one would be here. However, maybe this will work out for the better. I was told to leave a message behind by destroying a few personal items. What more prized items could I find than the professor's wife and daughter?" The man then crept closer to the frightened pair before adding, " Don't worry, total destruction won't be necessary. I'll just leave a little mark."

"Just tell me the message you want to leave and I can relay it for you."

"It's simple. The LPS has gone too far. They're out of their league and they need to quit the game, now!"

The man took two more steps and was now just a few feet away. "How nice though," he commented crudely. "A mother and daughter all dressed up pretty. Too bad they have to stay home." The trespasser then reached forward with his pistol and rubbed it in ominous, gentle strokes over Marina's cheek. He looked squarely into her eyes before turning his ill begotten stare slightly as he heard Colleen begin to sob louder.

"Don't cry, kitten. I'm sure your mother will enjoy this," he said stretching his left hand across the girl's face in a ghoulish caress.

At that moment Marina lunged into the man thrusting the kitchen knife that had been concealed behind her back deep into his side below the rib cage. The man winced in pain dropping the gun from his hand. He doubled over toppling down upon the weapon before Marina was able to intercept it so, instead, she grasped her daughter's wrist and stepped over the prone man. She located the small direct communication device she'd left on the counter before the two exited through the back door. They raced down the path into the orchard while Marina pushed the device's send button.

"Yes, dear," came the reply.

"A man's broken into the house!"

"What?"

"I said a man broke in," she repeated while trying to recapture her breath. "He has a weapon!"

"Where is he now?" Thomas Sanders asked anxiously.

"He's in the kitchen. We've escaped to the orchard."

"Good, find somewhere to hide. I'm almost home. Hang on the line while I call the police."

Meanwhile, the invader groggily pushed his body from the floor and was out the door in pursuit. Before entering the orchard he reached into his vehicle to retrieve a powerful flashlight that he used to scan the grounds behind the house. He then found the same path that Marina and Colleen had taken and followed like a wounded predator.

"Marina, Marina!" Tom called.

There was no response. Tom feared the worst. But finally a text message flashed across the screen. It read, "Can't risk talk. He's too close."

Tom sped up the driveway wheeling around to see the intruder's vehicle parked ominously in the rear of the house. He followed the same trail, which was so very familiar to him. Where would Marina hide, he wondered? She would probably go to the forest beyond the orchard. The trees were larger there and would provide a better hiding place. But maybe I shouldn't go there, he considered. I don't want to lead the thug right to them. But what if he's already there too? I need to help.

Marina and Colleen continued down the path to the small forest, hesitated, and then made their way along the tree line bordering the orchard some fifty yards before locating a large oak where they sought cover. The man was still behind them swinging his light from side to side into the rows of fruit trees until he too came to the forest. He stopped there and turned off his light. The man crouched down, resting, putting his hand to his side as he grimaced. He pulled the mask from his face to gather more oxygen.

Tom Sanders was searching for the flickering light he had noticed. It was gone now but he continued down the path until he reached the forest. Like the others he paused as if the abrupt change in flora triggered the brain to ask a question. How shall I proceed from here? Sanders didn't notice the man slumped against a tree a little ways from the path.

"I'm so glad you could make it home, Professor Sanders," the man said, taking in a labored breath.

Sanders jumped, redirecting his body toward the voice. "Who is it?" he asked unable to distinguish the outline of the man's face in the dark shadows.

"That's not important. What's important is that you need to understand that the LPS is officially out of business."

"Where are my wife and daughter?"

"Oh, they're out here somewhere and they're in better shape than myself. It seems your wife has some pent-up hostility that she decided to take out on me."

The man wheezed and again reached for his side. Sanders could sense that he was in great pain.

"Why don't we get you back to the house for some first aid and to where we can call for help?"

"No, professor! I was sent here to leave a message but your family has not been very receptive to cooperating. It seems possible that the only way I'll get through to you folks is by shooting one of you."

Marina heard the voices, one of which sounded like Tom's, so she snuck forward with Colleen at her side. She saw Tom standing looking down at the man sitting with his back to a tree. As she watched the man slowly rose to his feet with one arm extended pointing the same pistol at her husband that had been previously directed at her. Colleen finally looked up seeing what her mother was watching and gasped. Sanders turned his head slightly drawing the attention of the injured man who then gingerly picked up his light and shined it into the trees.

"Come out!" the man ordered.

There was no answer.

"Come out now or the professor will be shot."

"If you're out there stay in the trees," Sanders interrupted.

A shot rang out scalding the ground just to the side of Sanders' left foot. "That will be the only warning!"

Marina and Colleen slowly emerged from the trees and the gunman pulled his mask back over his face. "Okay. We're going to carefully make our way back to my vehicle during which time I'll be determining if one of you needs to be sacrificed. But, if I do nothing else, I still owe you a payback, Mrs. Sanders."

They began walking toward the house in single file: daughter first, then mother, father and gunman in the rear. When they were almost halfway back they heard sirens moving closer and then, shortly later, they saw flashes from police lights moving up the driveway. "Stop!" the gunman demanded. "You're going to have to lead me out in a different direction. Everyone turn around. The girl goes first again. Professor, you'll tell her where to go. Don't raise your voice too loud, though."

They changed positions. Colleen walked past her parents offering each a frightened, questioning glance. Marina walked past next giving her husband seemingly the same questioning expression as her daughter before she looked down to avoid eye contact with the gunman. He shoved her forward with his pistol when she reached his side. Then, as soon as he lowered the gun looking back for the professor to pass Sanders slammed his body into his pushing his fist into the wounded man's side. Sanders pounced atop the man as he fell inflicting another punch to the wound before the man rolled free.

The melee jarred the gun loose and Marina searched desperately in the area where she thought she saw the pistol fly off the path. Colleen screamed and rushed the man kicking at him while her father climbed to his feet. The man swung back at Colleen using his flashlight as a weapon. He hit her sharply above the knee and sent her crashing into a fruit tree as Sanders dove back on the man. The man was prone but now atop the pistol once more. He struggled to grasp it while pushing back against Sanders. He located the trigger and fired striking the professor and sending him reeling across the path.

The gunman struggled to his feet taking aim at Sanders as spotlights darted into the orchard. The man lowered his gun and turned scampering toward the forest under severe strain.

# Chapter 15

"How is he?"

"He lost a lot of blood but luckily none of his vitals were pierced so he'll be fine. They're just keeping him for observation. He could be released as soon as tomorrow."

"And Colleen?"

"She has a bad contusion above her knee and another on her back where she landed against the tree. She's a tough kid, a lot tougher than she likes to pretend. She'll be coming home with me tonight."

"I hope you'll have an armed guard!"

"Don't worry, we'll be fine. The police will be making regular check-ups on the house."

"Have they been able to tell you anything yet? Have they found the man?"

"I've been badgering them but still they're saying they have nothing," Marina declared. "It's hard to believe that with all their tracking technology that they've been unable to find a wounded man on foot."

"What about the vehicle?"

"It was rented with fake identification."

"That's possible?"

"So they say. Even harder to believe is that they can't find any fingerprints or other evidence in the vehicle. But there's gotta be something they're missing. I'm going to see if a couple of my old law school chums in the District Attorney's office can use their influence to push things along."

"Excuse me. Has anyone noticed that there's a patient in this room?" His wife's conversation with Tamara Hopkins had awoken Tom Sanders.

"I'm sorry, Tom," Tamara replied. "I shouldn't have been asking Marina so many questions."

"That's okay. I need to wake up and get out of this place anyway. From the sounds of it I think I'll be needing to take over the crime investigation."

"It scared me to death when I'd heard what happened."

"Indeed, that's why I need to find out who's behind this."

"Don't you think you should lay low and get some rest first? Let the police take care of this."

"That's exactly what they want. They want us to lay low and go out of business."

"Us?"

"Yes, I believe you're part of this too, Tamara. It seems that whoever did this has a vendetta out for the LPS."

"You think that's what this is about?" Tamara asked glancing toward Marina. When Marina had called with the news she only said that Tom had been shot saving her and Colleen from a home invader. She didn't want to get into too much detail over the phone and as a result Tamara assumed that, if the crime was premeditated, it somehow related to Marina's legal business.

"Maybe you two should talk privately for a few minutes," Marina suggested.

"Why?" Tom asked. "It's not like our society is a secret anymore."

"True but if I'm going to be asking a lot of questions of the police I'd feel better about not being able to answer any questions in return. I shouldn't know too much about what you people are up to," Marina responded as she excused herself from the room.

Tamara watched Marina exit to the hallway and then said, "I should have known. I'm so sorry. It's me that's stirred up all this trouble."

"Stop," Tom demanded quietly. "We're in this together. We knew that affecting change would have its risks."

"I'm the one who purchased Gardner's plum property at the auction and then wouldn't let Robert accept his offer to sell it to him. I'm also the one who introduced Arthur Flemming to the group. That thug should have been after me, not you."

"I'm not sure where you're going with this, Tamara, but remember that you were only the front woman for the acquisition. The society purchased the land and we all agreed to hang on to it."

"Yes, of course. But I've drawn too much attention to the society. I should have been more careful."

"Maybe the society needed more attention—well, maybe not this much attention," he responded while gazing down at his shoulder. "But let's back up to what you were saying about Gardner and Flemming. You believe they're the ones who want to put us out of commission and are behind this attack?"

"No, I trust Arthur. But he's Gardner's bitter rival. Gardner's upset that we got his property and, now, if he thinks Arthur is working with us he'd do anything to disrupt our plans."

"So you're clearly pointing the finger at Gardner?"

"Is there anywhere else to point it?"

Sanders didn't answer and an uncomfortable silence ensued as he surveyed the four walls of his hospital room. His initial bravado and eagerness to unravel the crime were subdued as he realized the dangers that remained. Then he asked, "What about the other council members? Do they know what's happened?"

"Yes. After Marina called I contacted the rest. They all wanted to come see you but we decided that it would be best if we weren't seen at the hospital."

"So what are you doing here then? I thought you said you needed to be more careful?"

"You know Andy's mad as hell. He wants to track down whoever's done this."

"You're changing the subject. Are you sure that no one has followed you here?"

A rap on the door sounded before Tamara offered a reply and a nurse poked her head into the room. "I'm sorry to interrupt but I need to do a check-up."

"That's okay," Tamara told her. "It was time for me to leave anyway."

# Chapter 16

Andy Cemanski wasn't quite sure that he'd heard the news correctly. The Rural Reformers were entering a candidate to challenge Nathan Coulter's regime. Coulter had been elected essentially unopposed for his last two terms so the chances that they'd unseat him were slim but at least someone was going to try.

"It's about time," the grizzled activist muttered to himself.

Andy knew the Rural Reformers candidate, Samuel Anthony, reasonably well because he had conferred with him on several joint objectives during previous campaigns. He respected Anthony; however, Andy wished that Samuel's sister, Carolyn, were the one running. Carrie was a more impressive speaker and a tireless advocate for land use reform. But they must have talked this through and figured that Sam would be the stronger candidate, Andy considered.

His next impulse was to offer whatever support he, or the LPS, could lend. If Sam were too busy to take his call, then maybe Carrie could provide a few suggestions on how Andy might assist the Rural Reformers' campaign. Andy was becoming more and more excited. He'd been downcast since learning that the Sanders' home was broken into and Tom had been shot, but this was a new light. A candidate, an entire organization was going to challenge his archenemy. What a crowning moment it would be if he were to see Nathan Coulter dethroned. There wasn't any real possibility of this happening but, nevertheless, the mere flickering hope brought a smile to Cemanski's battle weary face.

Tom Sanders had been released from the hospital and, for Marina's sake, was pretending to rest. But he was antsy; there were too many provisions to be made to compensate for his absence from the University. Plus he wanted to be heard from to curtail the gossip that was probably spreading over University chat lines about what had happened to him. Moreover, the LPS council needed to gather to discuss their reaction to the attack. Where though? Persistent surveillance, which was hopefully protective but not necessarily sympathetic to their cause, prevented Tom from convening the council at his place.

The professor mulled over various alternatives before remembering a memorial he'd visited near a small café. This gave him an idea and before long he called Tamara to organize the rendezvous.

"Are you sure you're ready for this?"

"Yes," Tom replied confidently. "We need to meet."

"Where?"

"There's a coffee shop in Stillman. I don't know if I'd consider it remote but it's still less populated in that area than in most of the eastern half. Tell them to be there on Sunday at ten a.m."

Andy Cemanski arrived in Stillman fifteen minutes early that morning. Before his wife died, he'd agreed to slow down and spend more time at home. But with her gone the house was quiet, his daughter and his son—now living in another state—were busy with their families and so Andy often grew restless. Not surprisingly, Andy was ready to spring into action at first cue.

Cemanski circled the block several times trying to detect whether the enemy had placed a watch on the cafe before he settled into a parking space a little ways up the road. He waited in his vehicle until he saw Tom Sanders enter the shop's front door. Sanders called the meeting and designated the site so Andy figured it'd be best if he let him walk in first to establish protocol. Jason McAlpin, Robert Sonnvoldt and Tamara Hopkins arrived not long after Sanders. They were all happy to see Sanders seemingly recovered and looking remarkably spry for a man who'd taken a bullet just nine days before. But their excitement was guarded, as they were more suspicious than ever about who might be watching.

"Don't worry," Sanders assured them. "I used this place as a central meeting ground for a study group a few years back. The coffee's great and it's served by salt of the earth employees. I'm sure they all just think you're part of the nerdy faculty at NIU. I hope none of you take insult from that."

"I've been called a lot worse," Andy retorted. "So let's get to business. Who do you think was behind this cowardly attack and what are we going to do about it?"

"I think the answer to the first part of your question is obvious," Robert Sonnvoldt responded.

The group stared at Sonnvoldt, remaining silent, expecting that he'd complete his declaration.

"Well, isn't it? It had to be GDC."

"They're a good suspect," Jason McAlpin offered.

"Robert's right," Tamara joined in. "Everything points to them. So the second part of Andy's question was, how do we respond?"

"I'm not sure we do," McAlpin answered. "We don't have the forces to counter this sort of strike. Besides we're a peaceful organization out to save what God created. We don't want to get into a war."

"Yeah, I think it's best that we lay low for a while. We've finally obtained some property so let's be happy with that, concentrate on accumulating more resources, and see if we can buy a few more less contentious plots."

"You actually think that strategy can work, Robert?" Andy Cemanski countered. "The property we've acquired won't be worth a damn after it's been surrounded by more tracts of ill-conceived housing developments and retail strips put up by the John Gardner's of the world."

"So what do you want to do, get into a gunfight with them?" Robert questioned in a more elevated tone as the cautiousness that permeated the group earlier had evaporated.

"Look, I'm not out for a mercenary mission any more than you are but if we lay low now we'll be doing exactly as they'd intended. We've talked about this. Our only chance at succeeding is by raising awareness and getting the public to demand a stop to what's happening to our land. Right now could be the perfect time. The Rural Reformers are making a serious run at next spring's election. We need to help them keep the pressure on."

Cemanski paused for a moment when his gaze met Tom's. Then he continued, " The last thing I want is to put anyone in danger but, on the other hand, we can't put our tails between our legs and hide. I think you know that too, Tom, otherwise you wouldn't have summoned us here — why did you call us here?"

"To have just this conversation, Andy. But I also wanted to show you something. So please everyone, finish your coffee. I want to take you up the block to visit a monument."

"You're taking us on a field trip, professor?" Tamara asked lightheartedly.

"I guess you could call it that."

And so they settled their tab and followed the professor out the door and up the street with much curiosity. Sanders led them to a small park where a tall monument was set on a hill in the center of the green. A dedication appeared on a tablet at the base of the monument. The inscription was dated May 14, 1832, and was entitled Stillman's Run. They all stared at the tablet before Robert quipped, "I thought that you were a professor of agrarian history. This stone documents the history of local warfare with the American Indian."

Sanders ignored Sonnvoldt's comment and looked toward Tamara and requested, "Can you please read it aloud for us, Tam?"

"Sure, if you'd like. It says, 'First engagement of the Black Hawk War. Two hundred and seventy-five Illinois Militiamen led by Major Isaiah Stillman were put to flight by Black Hawk and his warriors who demoralized the volunteers and a new army had to be called into the field. Captain John G. Adams and eleven other soldiers were killed.' The names of the twelve soldiers are listed."

Tom waited for a few moments after she was finished and then said, "I find something just slightly strange about that inscription. Do you notice anything, Jason?"

"Other than we're talking about an event that happened some two hundred plus years ago? No, I don't."

"What are you trying to teach us, professor?" Andy asked, somewhat amused by Tom's antics.

"Well, think about the point of view."

Tamara studied Tom's face searching for clues and then glanced back at the stone. Robert fidgeted next to her and read the inscription once more before declaring, "I give up. What's it mean—to you anyway?"

"I believe this epitomizes what we're up against. Black Hawk thought he was protecting the land and defending his people's way of life. But look who's memorialized here; the soldiers of the settlers who were encroaching on what he was trying to maintain. Most, if not all, of the soldiers were probably honorable men. But if you think about it, how was the claim of the land speculators for whom they were fighting any more righteous than that of Black Hawk's?"

"Point taken," Robert acknowledged. "But I doubt that the people of Ogle County often think about Black Hawk and his War anymore and if they do, they probably would still take the side of their twelve forefathers who lost their lives here."

"Exactly. That's what we're up against. Today, there are contemporary settlers like John Gardner, or the principals of Manetti Homes and Newton Residential, with loud voices who are able to convince their foot soldiers that people like us are nothing but a nuisance. They say that our call for careful, considered development just stands in the way of progress. People believe them and it's usually too late by the time they've realized what's been sacrificed in order that the modern day speculator could cash in on the relentless march of settlement."

"You seem to have omitted Arthur Flemming from your list of modern day speculators," Robert retorted through clenched teeth,

"Oh, but the worst of them all," Andy interceded "is none other than Nathan Coulter."

Tamara was listening to the discussion and still reflecting on where Tom meant to go with this topic. Finally she spoke. "Tom, does this tie us back to the property that Gardner purchased in the southwestern part of the county? Is that the burial ground for Black Hawk's people?"

"Tom sighed, "If it were only that simple." Then he added, "That's the other part of the problem that we're up against. You see, in another strange sense, it would be easier to galvanize around a man like Black Hawk. He's someone that can be revered but, unfortunately, usually as a vanquished warrior rather than for the causes he tried to defend. The burial grounds on Gardner's property are from a civilization a thousand or more years earlier; one that never fought the encroachment of European settlers. It's hard to say whether if the public finds out about what's under Gardner's property that they'll actually care."

"I'm still confused, Tom," Jason McAlpin said jumping back into the conversation. "The Indian burial ground isn't our only strategy for fighting sprawl and if it doesn't even connect to Black Hawk why the emphasis here?"

"I believe it to be helpful to consider how the enemy might think and how the vast majority of undecided might think. History can be a strong indicator of future events."

"So then are you saying we should lay low because if we put up too much of a fight we'll get chased out of here and be squashed just like Black Hawk?"

"You seem to be taking the pessimistic view, Jason. No, part of what I'm trying to say is that we can't go it alone. We need to build alliances and sway the undecided. Maybe we can work with more groups like the Rural Reformers to spread our message. And perhaps people such as Arthur Flemming really can come to understand our point of view if we present it properly."

"I for one agree with you," Andy piped in. "I'm off now to see how we might work with the Double R. Your lesson has been most provocative, professor, but it's time that we get the heck out of here. The neighbors must be beginning to notice us here. This rock hasn't received this much attention since these twelve sons of guns were laid to rest."

# Chapter 17

John Gardner called Julie Dubose into his office. "We're going back to see this Sonnvoldt character. It'll be just you and me. We'll leave the rest of the staff out of it for now."

"If you wish but I didn't accomplish much the first time and Lucas sure wasn't any help."

"You weren't persuasive enough."

"With all due respect, John, I don't think that was entirely the case. The issue was that Robert Sonnvoldt didn't have as much influence with Tamara Hopkins and the LPS that we had thought. I think it was *he* who wasn't persuasive enough. Sonnvoldt couldn't convince them to sell the property."

"The woman is his girlfriend, right? So I strongly believe we can still use Sonnvoldt as a lever. We just need to approach him from a different angle. We need to equip him with the information that allows him to be more persuasive." Then Gardner slowly leaned back in his chair and added, "Julie, you may find this hard to believe coming from me but, nine times out of ten, love and jealousy influence a man's decision more so than his greed for land or money."

Julie Dubose couldn't contain her smile before responding, "So you do have a softer side, John."

"I wouldn't necessarily jump to that conclusion; however, I do have an observant side. I think that if I provide Mr. Sonnvoldt with information that hits a certain nerve, a jealous nerve perhaps, he'll be much more convincing, or should I say disruptive, within the LPS circle. So let's go see if we can take advantage of what I've observed about human nature. If we can't get the land back from them at least we can break-up those silly games they've been playing."

Robert Sonnvoldt was preparing dinner on a warm, early autumn evening when he heard a quiet buzz emanating from the alarm he'd recently installed to detect encroachments over his lot line. He set down the mixing bowl he was working with and went to investigate the possible intrusion from his front room door, which he'd left open to capture the unseasonably mild breeze. Through the screen he saw that a vehicle had pulled up and a man and a woman were stepping into his driveway. Robert recognized the lady. She was the same neatly appointed black woman who had visited several weeks earlier. The accompanying man was not the same one who had been with her before. This man looked more comfortable in business attire and less a thug than her last partner. The visitors noticed Robert staring at them through the screen as they strolled up the walkway.

"Well, hello, Mr. Sonnvoldt," Julie Dubose offered first.

"Forgive me. It will come to me. Um, hello, Ms. Dubose," Robert replied.

"Very good, you remembered. I'm honored. Let me introduce you to my boss, John Gardner."

"Hello, Mr. Gardner. To what do I owe the pleasure of this call? It seems I've grown quite popular with the folks at GDC," Robert said, trying to hide his discomfort with the unexpected visit from these still unlikely guests.

"Julie says that you made a favorable impression upon her and I thought that I'd like to meet you for myself. I apologize for not making an appointment but we were in the neighborhood and I decided to take the chance that maybe you'd have a few moments for us."

"I was making dinner."

"Double apologies, but if you can bear with us our business won't take long."

"I don't think that I have any business with you, Mr. Gardner."

"Possibly not, but we do have mutual concerns."

"I thought that I'd made it pretty clear with Ms. Dubose that there's really nothing GDC and I have to offer to each other."

"Of course. But I would like to share my concerns with you," Gardner responded as he glanced toward the door latch subtly requesting an invitation inside.

Robert grew more nervous as he thought of the incident at the Sanders home. He didn't know what to make of the situation. Why was Dubose there with Gardner? Was she there to make the visit appear less threatening so that he'd relinquish his guard? Where was the thug? Certainly a man of Gardner's stature wasn't about to do his own dirty work.

"What are your concerns?" Robert asked curtly in attempt to mask his own concern, which was beginning to border on primal fear.

"If you don't mind let's sit down inside and have an open discussion. I think you'll understand why I'm troubled," Gardner replied calmly.

"You said your business wouldn't take long, so you can tell me what's on your mind from right where you're at," Sonnvoldt countered, his angst growing more apparent.

"I'm sorry if we make you feel uncomfortable, Robert," Gardner said before adding, "May I call you Robert?"

"Robert is fine and yes, you do make me feel uncomfortable."

"That's not our intention."

"Oh, but your reputation and the work of your thugs proceed you."

Gardner's eyes darted rapidly surveying Sonnvoldt's countenance, searching for his meaning before turning to Julie Dubose for translation. She raised her eyebrows and pursed her lips. She didn't seem to understand Sonnvoldt's inference either so Gardner turned back and responded directly, "I'm not sure what you've heard about my reputation or my work, Robert, but let me assure you that I hold no ill-feeling toward you. However, I sense that easing your concern with me may require that you get to know me better. That may take a little while so in the meantime, why don't I start by sharing my concern with you."

Robert considered Gardner's words carefully before consenting, "Go ahead."

"Sure, we wanted the eighty acres on Prairie Parkway that Ms. Hopkins took from us at the auction. I'm over that though. It's really small potatoes compared to the unseemly alliance that the LPS is getting itself into. Getting in bed, literally and figuratively, with Arthur Flemming is a dangerous game to play. Please, Robert, don't take my statement as a threat. I'm only trying to warn you to watch every move he makes. Flemming's a con artist."

"I'm not that familiar with the LPS and I have no idea who this Flemming is," Robert replied.

"I'm here to help you so we don't need to pretend with one another. Tamara Hopkins, Thomas Sanders, Jason McAlpin, good ole Andy Cemanski and yourself are the five members of the LPS governing council," Gardner stated bluntly. "Hopkins is sleeping with Flemming and, for whatever reason, she's introduced him to the council as an alleged ally. I don't know whether she's turned on you people or if she's just that naïve. But this could spell disaster for your entire organization."

Gardner artfully wove fact with what, to Robert, would seem plausible innuendo. Robert turned a ghostly pale as he stared through the screen. He consciously felt his throat constricting as Gardner continued speaking. "Do you understand what I'm trying to tell you or do I need to provide you with further detail of Flemming's background?"

Robert's lips tightened and he remained silent.

"Mr. Sonnvoldt, are you okay?" Julie Dubose inquired.

Robert turned his head slowly to face her. "Yes, Ms. Dubose, I'm okay," he finally replied. Then he paused again before saying, "But I don't understand why Mr. Gardner is telling me this and why he'd bother to offer a warning. You people don't give a damn about the LPS."

"I won't tell you that I agree with everything that the LPS does. Nonetheless, I get the feeling that most of your people are well intentioned. Therefore, I can live with the LPS. It's people like Arthur Flemming that frighten me. He's using your organization as cover to expand his evil empire into Ogle County."

The comments registered slowly upon Robert but he didn't bother to ask for details. At the moment he couldn't bear to hear anymore. Instead he said, "I think that I need to check on my dinner."

"I understand. We've inconvenienced you enough already this evening so we'll be leaving. Contact me if you need any more information about Flemming. You can probably figure out how to reach me so there's no reason to leave you my card. Have a nice dinner," Gardner concluded as he nodded to Julie Dubose and they turned back toward the driveway.

While pushing the start button Gardner turned to Dubose again and remarked, "Sonnvoldt's not a very charming fellow. As a matter of fact," the development mogul continued as they drove away, "he seems pretty strange. I wonder how he ever managed to attract the Hopkins woman's interest?"

# *Chapter 18*

Colors were ablaze across the leafy campus inspiring academic thought and offering a welcome respite from the surrounding landscape rendered sterile by unending, indistinguishable tracts of development devoid of town square, pasture or woodlot. As he strolled along its walkways Professor Sanders felt fortunate to find his milieu on the institution's grounds. The architecture didn't conjure visions of Ivy League schools founded centuries earlier but the University's properties had been preserved and renovated unlike most commercial and residential structures that had been replaced by new development and left behind to decay. The fact that Northern Illinois University had survived and continued to flourish was not lost on the professor. As state governments weakened and funding dried up similar public universities throughout the country had floundered. Proximity to Chicago, still one of the nation's academic and cultural centers, fostered necessary regional concern and substantial endowment reserves helped guide the institution through the worst of the public education crisis. During this period, DeKalb County officials were only too happy to assist the university with generating liquidity via divestiture of excess land holdings. Not surprisingly, as years passed, the majority of students, faculty and staff referred to the school as DeKalb University even though the official charter remained Northern Illinois University.

Over the well-traveled promenade past the main library, several academic halls and administrative offices the professor veered onto a narrower path that led to the university archives. The record building was subtle as a result of its tucked-away location yet stately in appearance. Letters engraved in the stone above the arched entrance read, "These archives bridge past, present and future." Rather a bold statement, the professor thought, for the face of a building whose contents few other than historians would find at all interesting. The professor presented his palm to pass security in order to proceed into the main hall where he stopped to admire stacks of books and records held behind a low marble railing. He still had several minutes before his ten o'clock appointment with Ross Lieberman, the Curator of Archives.

Sanders considered the irony of such a vast collection of paper in the current age of information transport and storage; however, there was a need for the hard copy that went beyond Lieberman's obsession with antiquity. Electronic storage, imaging systems, holograms and various other technologies had been evolving in some form or another for one hundred years. Nevertheless, the newest advancements were eventually conquered by a hack intent on destroying or altering data. The curator was so concerned about the destruction of key records that he would only permit access to certain databases from designated ports within the archives building. The paper documents provided the last line of defense. "God help us if we ever need them," Lieberman once told Sanders.

Suddenly, Sanders felt a hard slap across his back. Still jittery from the recent attack at his home, he took one step forward, whirled and turned to face his assailant.

"My, Tom, did you have one too many cups of coffee this morning? You're a bit jumpy."

The professor was now staring directly at the aging curator. "I'm sorry, Ross. You scared the wits out of me. How long have you been standing there?"

"Not long. I saw you coming down the path from my office window. I thought I'd come down to greet you personally."

The professor was not an uncommon visitor and he and the curator had developed a friendly relationship over the years. Despite coming off as quite the curmudgeon upon first impression, Lieberman had been ever so helpful with numerous data searches during Sanders tenure at the university. The professor could research from his office or home but there was certain information that Sanders could only gain access to by visiting the archives. Beyond that, by enlisting Lieberman's expertise he was able to reduce what would have taken him days to find on his own down to just a few hours. The archives carried many more records than just those that had been generated at the university and Sanders found the curator to be particularly useful at ferreting out the ownership chain of properties.

Most recently, before the home invasion, Sanders had asked for Lieberman's assistance to research the title chain related to certain Ogle County properties. Initially Sanders was reluctant to ask for help. The project went beyond the scope of the professor's normal farm property research and he was afraid to involve the curator in something that could potentially be linked back to the LPS. But there was no other way. Sanders had reached a dead end on the Ogle County properties and Lieberman could direct him back to the database where the desired information could be retrieved.

"So, Tom, where have you been? I've heard you've been away from campus for the last couple of weeks."

"Yeah, I apologize for not calling but I was a little under the weather and decided that it would be best to work from home. I'm feeling much better now though."

"Well, while you were gone I decided to follow-up on some of the items you had requested. I've got quite a bit for you to pore through. If you'll follow me upstairs I've already set up a record search for you in an office down the hall from mine. I'll be close by in case you need more help as you proceed along."

Tom was curious to find what Lieberman had pulled together and, then, once he started to review the data he marveled. Before him was essentially every land transaction in Ogle County going back for hundreds of years. More importantly, Lieberman had set-up an easy to use search menu such that Sanders could instantly hone in on specific properties, buyers, sellers or types of transactions. The professor was particularly interested in deals involving John Gardner or GDC and those with certain zoning variances. As he went along he grew more and more comfortable with search procedures and eventually became curious about transactions involving other individuals, most notably Arthur Flemming. Sanders became immersed in the data. After several hours Lieberman stepped back in the office and said, "You've been awful quiet in here. I take it you're finding everything you need."

"Oh yes, Ross. What you've provided here has been most helpful. I'm ever so grateful to you."

"Good to hear but why don't you give your eyes a rest and join me for lunch."

"Um, oh, I hope it doesn't seem rude but I'd rather skip lunch today. I'm starting to make some progress here and I'd hate to lose my momentum."

"Suit yourself but Mrs. Lieberman's boy doesn't plan on skipping any meals," the portly curator said as he rubbed his belly.

"I'll stop by next week, Ross, and lunch will be on me."

Thereafter, Sanders pored over record after record losing all track of time. Lieberman finally poked his head into the room again at a little after five o'clock. "Look, I know that you're having fun but this old man needs to get home."

Glancing at his watch Tom responded, "I'm so sorry. I didn't realize that the afternoon had slipped away."

"No problem. Angela can see you out before she locks up. But don't push her. She'll get crabby if you keep her here much past six."

"Don't worry. I'll start wrapping up and will be ready to go soon."

When Lieberman left Tom Sanders sat back, considered everything that he had reviewed in the records that day and muttered, "I'd expect it from some of those guys but not him. I knew he was self-serving and ruthless but I didn't know he was a crook."

# Chapter 19

"I haven't been this excited in years. I feel like a young Turk again, like I'm in my thirties. Finally it feels like we're back in the war."

"Tell me about it, Andy. I have the bullet wound to prove we're in a war."

"Well, sorry about that part of it, Tom. Those land purchases really riled up John Gardner. I never thought the bastard would go to that extent to get back at us. But, anyway, I just had a chat with Carrie Anthony. From the way she talked, it sounds like her brother will make a formidable candidate and that the Rural Reformers have a well crafted campaign strategy. They may not have a snowball's chance of unseating Nathan Coulter but they will have the opportunity to stick a few pins into little Napoleon's side. What do you say we get together back at that coffee shop you took us to so I can fill everyone in on what Carrie's told me?"

"Okay because I might have a few things to report that will interest you as well, Andy."

"Like?"

"Like some tidbits involving your good friend Mr. Coulter, or Emperor Napoleon as you refer to him."

"Oh yeah," Cemanski responded quizzically. "What you got?"

"We'll talk about it at Claire's. That way the entire council can hear."

"Who's Claire?"

"The coffee shop."

"Oh, right."

After disconnecting Andy grew more curious about the information that Tom Sanders had picked up concerning Nathan Coulter. It must be something juicy, Andy thought, for Sanders to have brought it up. Tom knew the degree to which Andy loathed Coulter so he wouldn't toy with him when it came to matters surrounding the County Clerk's escapades.

Oh well, Andy resolved, I can wait for the news. There were other issues to occupy his mind considering that in the span of less than two months the LPS had acquired two parcels of land, a potential enemy, Arthur Flemming, had become an ally and now the Rural Reformers had announced that they were mounting a challenge to unseat Nathan Coulter in next spring's county election.

The Rural Reformers, or Double R as they were also known, had put up candidates before but were never able to amass many votes. "Bleeding hearts that are all talk with nothing to offer the general public," is how Coulter described them. But after talking to Carrie Anthony, Andy was convinced that this time could be different. Double R had research and responses that would contradict Coulter's unfounded claims.

"Development was good for the economy," Coulter stated. "The Rural Reformers want to restrict your standard of living," he warned.

"Whose standard of living?" the Rural Reformers were ready to rebut. Carrie Anthony told Andy about the impact study that Double R commissioned relative to the last two mega-developments completed in Ogle County. The findings concluded that the only people who had improved their economic status as a result of these projects were a select few developers. The new housing was actually wreaking havoc on certain home prices further east. The new commercial developments drove several existing establishments out of business and produced a net decrease in overall business profits in the affected area. Numerous abandoned buildings and unpaid rents were left in the wake of these projects.

"Oh, but their study includes what happened in DeKalb, Kane and other counties," Coulter would counter.

"So what are we supposed to do?" Carrie asked. "Bask in our good fortune at the expense of our neighbors? Anyone who responds yes is short sighted. What's happening elsewhere will occur here on the county's east side in a matter of time. We need area-wide cooperation. Does it really matter if our commercial strips are newer and bigger than theirs?"

"Do you want to hear another one of Coulter's fallacies?" Carrie asked.

"Lay it on," Andy replied with widening eyes.

"New development will reduce taxes!" Her voice quivered and her eyes gleamed as she stated what was the County Clerk's argument. "Bunk, I say to that!" she opposed. "Taxes never have and never will be reduced given the lack of planning and given all the concessions he grants to his developer buddies. More houses and more retail strips mean more roads, more clean up, more police, more everything. These things cost money and who pays for it? The average taxpayer that's who. Oh yeah, and don't forget that we'll need to set aside funds to drill our wells another couple hundred feet deeper when the next development comes along and sucks our water table dry."

Carrie was becoming even more animated. "Let's forget about the money part for a moment. Let's talk about what all of this development has done for our quality of life. We're not rural, we're not small town but, on the other hand, we're not big city. They say you can't have the best of both worlds; however, it seems we haven't the best of either. We've lost the pleasure of watching the brook run swiftly through the meadow in springtime. Glimmers of fresh fallen snow glistening on forest trees are hard to come by. When's the last time you tried to pull your vehicle off to the side of a country road to observe the sun set over an open pasture? If you did you were probably sideswiped by an angry commuter in a hurry to get home. Most of us barely recognize our neighbors. And for what we've lost, in return, have we received the cultural benefits of the big city? I would say not. There's no live theater, no orchestras in Ogle County. When's the last time you've seen an art exhibit or been to a museum in your hometown? We've neither the charm of a small town nor the culture of a big city. Instead, we've metamorphosed into one nondescript, sterile community."

Later on, Andy remembered feeling a strong urge to kiss Carrie when she had finished speaking. He hoped that her brother could inspire his constituency half as well as she had moved him. Now, he wanted to tell the LPS council members about what he had heard. They, in turn he would recommend, needed to spread the word to the general membership and so on down the line.

Meanwhile, as Andy recounted his meeting with Carrie Anthony, Tom was calling to assemble the council. The last member to be contacted was Robert Sonnvoldt. Sonnvoldt seemed to be expecting Tom's call. In spite of that, he was absorbed in his own thoughts, hearing yet not comprehending what Sanders was saying. "I'm sorry, what was that you said?"

"I said we needed to get together to discuss the Rural Reformers' campaign."

"I can't."

"This is important, Robert. When would be a convenient time for you? I'm sure the others can juggle their schedules if necessary."

"I mean I can't, not with *her* there, anyway."

Tom instantly understood Robert's lament. "Look, Robert, I don't know what's gone on between you and Tamara. That's your business but this is a professional matter so you need to put your personal feelings aside. You have responsibilities as a council member."

"It's more than just me personally that I'm concerned about. She's deceived us, the LPS."

"What are you talking about?"

"She's sleeping with Flemming. They're using us to gain ground in Ogle County."

"Come on, Robert. You can't be serious."

"I wish I wasn't."

"I understand that your break-up with Tamara could have been painful. After going through a relationship loss your mind can play awful tricks on you, it can translate hard feelings into negative thoughts. You'll get past this though."

"See, Tom, you've seen what's happening too. How would you have known Tamara and I broke up?"

"No, I haven't seen anything other than the friction between the two of you at the last few council meetings. So what is it, Robert? Have you overheard their conversations or seen a note that leads you to the conclusion that they're out to deceive us?"

"No, but I've been told."

"By whom?"

"Gardner."

"Excuse me."

"John Gardner told me."

Sanders took pause, flabbergasted. Had Sonnvoldt gone mad? Had the loss of such an incredible woman as Tamara driven him off the deep edge? Sanders recovered from his lack of words and asked, "What dealings do you have with John Gardner?" Then, not waiting for a reply he added, "Whatever they may be, how could you find anything the man said to be credible? The man almost had me killed!"

"It wasn't him."

"What? How do you know that?"

"I could tell by what he said and the way he looked at me. I don't think he even realizes that you were shot."

"It only makes sense that it was one of Gardner's thugs."

"Maybe that's exactly what Flemming wants you to think."

The professor was stunned. He didn't know if there was any basis in what Sonnvoldt was suggesting but his comments made Tom's mind race.

"Okay, Robert. Let's meet before the other council members arrive so that we can talk this through."

"I won't go to the meeting, Tom. What are we doing anyway? We're not politicians. We don't need to discuss strategy or campaigns or anything like that. We're in way over our heads already."

"We need to talk. We're not going to give up after all we've been through."

"You're right but we do need to realign our focus. Let's muster our resources and buy some more properties over in the northwest corner. The LPS can create a sanctuary out there."

# Chapter 20

Predictably, Andy Cemanski arrived at the coffee shop first. This time he didn't wait for Tom Sanders before entering the small café. Quaint, he thought, as he looked over the shop searching for a table that would be out of the earshot of other patrons.

"Well hello, professor. I'm glad you decided to come back."

Cemanski looked over his shoulder expecting to see Sanders coming through the door before realizing that the waitress was speaking to him. "Um, good afternoon, Ma'am," he responded turning back toward the petite woman with graying hair.

"Ma'am? I beg your pardon. I doubt if I'm a day older than you are, professor. Why don't you call me Minnie?"

"Sure, no problem, Minnie," Andy replied with a wink.

"Where's professor Tom been hiding you all these years anyway? I think there's a chance that you might be just my type."

"What type is that?"

"The type that's slowed down a bit so that I can catch 'em."

Andy was starting to enjoy the flirting, even if it meant putting up with being cast as a professor. He couldn't risk telling the lively waitress why he was really at the cafe; better that she thought he was there for a meeting of academicians. He never knew who was listening and when enemies of the LPS might be close at hand. So rather than trying to explain, Andy went on to shower Minnie with folksy witticisms until eventually being interrupted by Tom Sanders.

Sanders had been standing behind Andy for several moments eavesdropping on their conservation before projecting a stammer. "Eh hem, excuse me. Do you mind if I join you?"

Minnie answered first. "Not at all, professor. I love it when men fight over me."

Tom laughed but Andy blushed as he realized the professor had caught him with the tough guy image he preferred to wear folded neatly and stashed away. "I didn't mean to step into the middle of anything here," Sanders jabbed. "I can leave you two alone if you'd like to chat some more in private, Andy."

Cemanski just turned redder until his innocently awkward moment was relieved by the arrival of Jason McAlpin. Seeing McAlpin stroll up was Minnie's cue to tend to other customers. "I'll be back after you get settled," she called over her shoulder. "You gents can draw straws because I don't know how I'm gonna be able to choose between the three of you."

"What's this all about?" Jason asked as Minnie flitted away.

"Tell him," Tom chuckled.

"Never mind," Andy replied. "Let's take a seat and wait for the others."

Before long Tamara joined the men and they all began sipping their first cups of coffee. Putting the earlier banter behind, Andy was anxious to get to business. "Where's Robert? Did he forget about our meeting?" he asked directing his question Tamara's way.

"I don't know," Tamara responded raising her eyebrows and tightening her lips in a manner meant to imply, "How should I know?"

Sanders studied his friend's demeanor searching for clues in her eyes. Was she surprised that Robert hadn't shown up? But before letting the others curiosity linger Tom said, "Robert called to tell me that he won't be attending our meeting today."

"Why not?" Andy barked.

"He said that he's not comfortable with our agenda."

"How could he be uncomfortable with our agenda? We're developing strategy to defend open lands. That's our mission."

"His words in a nutshell were that he thinks we've become too political and that we're out of our league when it comes to dealing with politicians. He wants us to refocus." Sanders left out Sonnvoldt's accusation that Tamara was betraying the LPS.

"Hell, I'm not too fond of politicians myself but what are we supposed to do? Just let them roll over us? And now, … now we have a chance to align ourselves with some politicians who might be on our side for a change and who might actually help us fight the bad guys," Andy seethed before redirecting to Tamara. "What do you know about Robert's aversion to politics?"

Again Sanders looked to study Tamara's response, her body language. Did anything indicate that Tamara Hopkins wasn't exactly who he thought she was? Was there anything to indicate that Robert Sonnvoldt's account had any merit? But prior to Sanders being able to read into Tamara's countenance, Andy continued his questioning.

"What's Robert's vision of refocusing?"

"Excuse me," Tom said turning back toward Andy.

"What does Robert want us to do?"

"He thinks we should develop a sanctuary up in the northwest corner of the county starting with the land he won at the auction."

"Ridiculous. What's he thinking? How much land could we really purchase up there? We'd be on a tiny island while Coulter let Gardner and the rest of the bunch pave the entire rest of the county right around us."

"I understand that but there was no way of explaining it to Robert," Tom responded glancing across to Tamara again. "Not in the mindset he was in anyway," the professor added.

"I'll explain it to him." Andy clenched his teeth, … "but later. I want to brief Jason and Tamara about what I learned about the Rural Reformers' campaign first."

Without further delay Andy went on to provide a rather thorough explanation of the Rural Reformers' platform. Cemanski's analysis was so detailed with regard to certain issues that Tom speculated that Andy must have been filling in his own blanks and assuming that the Double R would handle matters just as he'd see fit. There's no way Andy could have picked up and retained this much information in the less than hour long conversation he'd had with Carrie Anthony, the professor thought. Cemanski spent a particularly long while explaining how the government, under Double R's watch, would reform the way it dealt with developers. Everything would be above board and the public would be made aware of any special concession made to a developer. "Fact is," Andy exclaimed, "there shouldn't be any concessions period. Why should we allow our land to be stripped away for the sake of making a few guys rich? Short sighted greed is what we've been up against all along."

Tom wondered what Tamara was thinking when Andy expounded on about making real estate transactions even more transparent than they supposedly were now. Had she learned about the shady land deals her new partner had been involved with? Certainly Arthur Flemming wouldn't be one who'd benefit from more public disclosure.

Andy continued by describing the credentials of Samuel Anthony, the Rural Reformers' candidate for County Clerk. "He's not like some of the milk toast candidates they've put up in the past. He has charisma."

"That'll be a nice change for once," Jason McAlpin commented.

"Yes. But I wish his sister was in the race," Andy lamented. "Even more so than her brother, I think she has what it takes to step up and hit Coulter with the knockout punch!"

Tamara, who had been quietly, intently listening through Andy's dissertation on the Double R and the upcoming campaign, finally spoke. "I can see you're excited about next spring's election, Andy, and I'm not so sure that you wouldn't make a good candidate for the Double R yourself but, in the meantime, what should the LPS be doing to help?"

"We need to get out the votes. We need to start an old-fashioned grass roots campaign!"

"That sounds good but remember that our organization is currently banned from public demonstration. Remember, Coulter convinced the Court that we're subversives."

"I know. That SOB! Well, the LPS might be banned as a group but our members, or should I say our sympathizers, are still registered voters. As the council we need to personally meet with each and every one of them to make sure that they understand the significance of this campaign. Each member ..., er sympathizer, should spread the word to their own personal network as well and make sure they get out the vote. If everyone makes an effort this can all be done through private communication. No public demonstrations will be necessary."

Andy proceeded to ramble on for several more minutes. Alternately confident that if the LPS worked hard enough they could make a difference in the election and, then, realistic in knowing that Coulter's power base was so strong that the Double R hardly stood a chance. No matter; for to Andy, like an aged knight riding to his last battle, carrying the banner with pride and putting up a good fight for all those who would follow to bear witness was just as important as the outcome that would be had on the field that day. Now, Andy's face was flush again and his speech became deliberate finally conscious, though not displeased, that he had dominated the group's discussion. He stopped talking entirely to survey the countenance of each of his compatriots. Satisfied that they understood his message he leaned in to Tom and said, "Now I know you had something you wanted to share with the group as well, so I'll try to be quiet for a while and listen to what you've to say."

"Thanks, Andy," Tom said and then fell silent. As a professor he was accustomed to public speaking and delivering his findings to a group but at the present he felt uncomfortable. Perhaps it was because this seemed so personal. He had dug up information on the nemeses that Andy Cemanski had just spoken of with such passion. Or maybe it was the doubt that Robert Sonnvoldt had placed in his mind. If Robert's accusation was true, then perhaps he shouldn't divulge what he was about to say in front of Tamara. Tom felt perspiration begin to bead on his forehead.

"I did some research," he finally started.

"Um, that's part of your job, isn't it?" Tamara interjected sarcastically.

Her comment wasn't unusual. Over the last several years Tamara had grown comfortable trading good-natured barbs with the professor. But today, Sanders was too tense to be able to extract any humor from her interruption.

"What I mean is that I've researched land contracts and purchases in Ogle County and have found a few interesting items," Sanders responded sounding uncharacteristically annoyed. "I've run across several unusual zoning variances granted on the eve of certain major land transactions."

"Give us an example, Tom," Andy anxiously requested.

"Well one of the most intriguing involves none other than John Gardner and Nathan Coulter. I think you're all familiar with the Majestic Point development."

"Sure," Jason replied, "but I didn't know that it was one of Gardner's projects."

"It's not; however, if we trace the land title back ten years something looks very peculiar. There's a forty-acre plot that lies square in the central entrance to Majestic Point that was originally owned by the Herbert family. At one time, the Herbert family farmed over two thousand acres and had another five hundred acres in river bottom and woodland. Much of the land was divided up through an estate plan and eventually Daniel Herbert was the only remaining family member who owned any significant acreage. Daniel still lived on a plot that Majestic Point later swallowed. He also still owned two hundred acres further west. The land around the forty acres where he resided had become increasingly residential and commercial and he fought off numerous offers from developers to purchase his property. As a matter of fact, I found a news article in which Herbert is quoted as saying he was hounded by developers and that he appealed directly to the then newly-elected Nathan Coulter to put an end to the harassment."

"I'm sure Coulter was a bundle of help," Andy commented cynically.

"Well, at that time, so it appeared" Tom answered. "You see, although Daniel was the only one left with land he certainly didn't inherit the Herbert family's best farming genes. And certainly, he wasn't one of their better businessmen. Records show that Daniel was being assessed tax on the forty-acre parcel at a rate as high as the nearby residential property owners even though he should have been entitled to a farmstead credit. Then he goes three years without paying his taxes and is on the verge of being evicted. The Clerk intervened saying 'the government couldn't simply turn their back on a common landowner with a long family history in Ogle County and throw him out of his home.' So Coulter arranged for an interest free loan under a two-year plan to allow Daniel to pay his back taxes. Of course the Clerk's general decree made press but the details of the agreement remained in the dark."

"So Herbert was obviously evicted in due time," McAlpin interjected.

"Not officially. The details of Coulter's plan with Herbert included finding a private third party to provide the loan that paid the taxes. The government prefers to be a borrower rather than a lender so it only made sense that a third party was brought in to make the loan to Herbert. The party agreed to make the loan provided that if it was not repaid in two years he'd have the right to assume title to the property."

"I think I only need one guess at who that third party was," Andy snarled.

"You got it. Then, of course, Herbert couldn't make the loan payment seeing as his ability to farm his other two hundred acres were diminishing and he had no other income sources."

"There's something I'm missing," Jason interposed again. "If Gardner is this third party that you seem to imply then why isn't his name plastered all over the Majestic Point development?"

"That's a reasonable question, my friend. What happened though is that the forty-acre parcel was immediately turned over to Ballinger Builders who desperately wanted it in order to start developing Majestic Point. Ballinger, in return, essentially gave Gardner a property further west that was four times the size."

"Didn't Ballinger think it was strange that Gardner had come to own the forty-acre parcel that they wanted? Furthermore, wouldn't they have been reluctant to trade a piece that was so much larger?" Tamara queried.

"Ballinger knew that they had a winner with Majestic Point and probably wasn't sure how long it would be before they could develop the parcel they gave up. And, to your first point, they probably didn't even know that they were dealing with Gardner. As I mentioned, the details of Coulter's bail out agreement with Herbert two years previously had never really been analyzed. I said Ballinger 'essentially' gave Gardner the larger, western property but the land swap was officially consummated with Herbert according to the documents. So after the swap, Gardner or Coulter or both of them were smart and they lay in the weeds. Then, Gardner purchases the larger parcel from Herbert at a price well below market value. No doubt this had been the prearranged resolution to the bail out agreement."

"So what's happened to the—let's see—one hundred and sixty acres that Gardner took over?"

"It just so happened that this property was adjacent to the other two hundred acres that Daniel Herbert still owned. Within a year Herbert sold that land to Gardner as well. The area was still in the rural belt of the county at the time but Gardner Development received a variance to build a subdivision across much of the land as long as they left eighty acres open as a working farm. You've heard of Daniel's Crossing haven't you?"

"Daniel's Crossing as in Daniel Herbert?"

"Gardner probably figured he owed him at least that much."

"I've always wondered how they come with the names for those subdivisions," Jason remarked. "But I drive by that area quite often; however, I can't remember having ever seen a working farm there."

"Well there's a maintenance shed, small landfill and a pen containing two goats on a portion of the property. I guess that's what they call their working farm."

"Whatever happened to Daniel Herbert?" Tamara asked.

"I managed to track down one of Daniel's cousins the other day. She said she still couldn't believe that he sold the property, particularly to a developer. She told me he moved to Georgia and that she hadn't heard from him since. So I did a quick check of Georgia's census records and found he died within three months after moving there."

"Bastards!" Andy exclaimed. "What else have they done?"

Sanders went on to detail three more out of the ordinary land deals involving well-known developers. Coulter's name wasn't entwined with these more recent transactions like it had been with the series of events surrounding the Herbert property. "However Coulter's involvement shouldn't automatically be dismissed," Tom cautioned. "The absence of his name may only be an indication of the Clerk's increasingly cunning political skills as the years passed."

"I can vouch for his abilities in that regard," Andy affirmed.

There were unusual circumstances related to a fifth land purchase that drew the professor's attention when he was at the university archives. This last one happened to involve Arthur Flemming and as Tom gazed over toward Tamara he decided not to share what he'd learned with the group. "Let's adjourn," he declared. "Let's absorb what's been discussed today and leave the formulation of action plans for tomorrow."

# Chapter 21

Thomas Sanders sat staring at the orchard visible from his den window. Cold weather was closing in and the trees were almost barren now. He was deep in thought and hadn't noticed Colleen enter the room.

"Dad, do you think he'll come back?" Her voice startled him.

"Excuse me."

"Do you think the burglar will come back to our house?"

"No, honey. He won't be back."

"How do you know?"

"The man was looking for something and he's figured out that he's not going to find it here. So he won't be back."

"I still get scared sometimes. I wish they'd catch him."

"I know, honey. I wish they'd catch him, too, but you don't have to worry. We've taken extra precaution to make sure that you're safe."

Marina caught the tail end of their conversation as she was passing by the room. She stopped and added her own reassuring words for her daughter. "Dad's right, Coll. We're safe now. You needn't worry."

"Okay then I guess I don't have any more excuses for not finishing my homework. I'm going back up to my room."

They watched their daughter head down the hall and when Marina felt that Colleen was far from earshot she said, "I'm frustrated, Tom. There's been one helluva stonewall erected at the P-O-C-I. Finding out anything further about our intruder friend has proved to be very difficult. I mean, come on, it seems like it's been months already."

"Excuse me, counselor. Go back for a second. You're dealing with a layman here. What's the P-O-C-I?"

"The Police Office of Criminal Investigations."

Until Colleen brought up her concern over the home invasion again Tom hadn't thought about the incident in some time. He'd been too busy worrying about his newest crisis. News concerning the Rural Reformers and finding information that could possibly be used to exploit chinks in the current political regime's armor was encouraging; however, this latest problem overshadowed that. One of the five members of the LPS council had all but officially resigned and while so doing had implicated Sanders' closest associate in an act of betrayal. Sanders wouldn't accept the latter part without further evidence but, nevertheless, Robert's insinuation bothered him. How could he find out whether there was any bearing of truth in what Robert told him? Part of Sanders wanted to completely dismiss what Robert said because, after all, Tamara was a dear friend and a trusted ally and it was very plausible that Robert's words were those of a scorned man lashing out at his former lover. Besides, Tom had already confronted Tamara once regarding the nature of her relationship with Flemming. But alas, he'd never been able to completely resolve how Arthur Flemming had suddenly, almost mysteriously, entered the picture via Tamara's introduction. There remained just enough doubt.

As Sanders gazed at his wife he considered asking for her advice. He respected her opinion immensely and perhaps she could offer sage counsel on handling his dilemma. How could he find out whether Tamara had really turned to the wrong side without, if she were innocent, destroying their trust and friendship? But no, he couldn't request Marina's advice. The situation had grown too complicated and with what Tom had learned about Coulter he'd risk compromising Marina's objectivity when it came to her legal work involving county matters. They'd always agreed that it was best that Marina knew as little as possible about the inter-workings of the LPS. Sanders determined that there was only one way to resolve his inner turmoil. He had to be direct and just as before ask Tamara what was going on between her and Flemming.

# Chapter 22

All three transactions transpired under similar circumstances and Andy, Jason and Tamara made a pact to divvy them up whereby each would dig into the details of one of the deals. Tamara chose a transaction, or actually a series of events, that started rolling when a so-called farmer named Jonas Waters purchased a sizable chunk of real estate at the county auction six years ago. Now, Tamara was attempting to recall every bit of information the professor had covered at their meeting.

"The property purchased by Jonas Waters was listed as rural under the county's land classification system exactly like the other two properties I told you about," Sanders had relayed at the café. Even though Ogle County had been converted to a residential and business county under the federal system, farms and open lands initially maintained a rural zoning classification. Property buyers were then required to maintain the property according to its classification until a change in status was approved via public order or referendum. This was supposedly intended to facilitate an orderly transition to the county's new overriding "Mixed-Use" designation.

The rural status of the Waters' property explained why Jonas had no competition from the developer contingent when he bid on the land at auction. However, within a year of his purchase Waters filed for hardship and was allowed to sell off a piece of land, representing about five percent of the total tract, under an emergency sale provision. The hardship and emergency sales provisions were rarely needed because bidders were required to submit financial information up front to support their assertion that they had the wherewithal to complete the purchase and adequately maintain the property thereafter. However, acknowledging the possibility that a buyer's financial position could deteriorate after purchase, the county provided for hardship cases and left leeway for assisting landowners with emergency sales of all or, in each of the cases that Sanders brought to light, parts of their property. Under the emergency provisions notice and auction procedures could be waived.

"You guessed it," Sanders had told them at the café, "the white knight who bought the small piece of property was a developer, in each case."

Due to the emergency nature of the sales no competitive bidding took place. The amount of land involved in all three sales was relatively small, averaging less than twenty acres, so public visibility wouldn't have been high anyway. "What happened then," Sanders informed the council, "was that the small piece of land was developed with little fanfare. In two cases, small residential neighborhoods were built, no more than twelve to fifteen houses. On the third, a small retail strip was constructed."

"Here's the truly amazing part though," the professor exclaimed. "Not long after the small developments were completed the zoning classification on the remaining large tracts flipped from rural to either residential or mixed use. Done just like that with no public notice, no referendum, no nothing."

"I've looked at the Jonas Waters title a hundred times," Tamara remembers Sanders saying. "One year the property is designated as rural and the next year it's not. There's absolutely no transactional record to document the change."

Two years after the rural designation was removed from the land purportedly owned by Waters, a major development was started. Title to the land was eventually subdivided and transferred to various homeowners and commercial landlords as development was being completed. However, the professor was unable to verify whether Waters ever received the proceeds from the sale of the subdivided plots.

"My guess," Tom said, "is that once the small development went up on the property carved out in the emergency sale, the public became accustomed to seeing houses and buildings there and forgot that the overriding designation on the main tract was still rural. Then, major development began and nobody thought to look back at the record books."

Sanders words echoed in her ears. "There's no evidence that Waters ever received the proceeds from the land sales." Well that's the obvious start, Tamara thought. Find Jonas Waters and see how much he's willing to discuss. He was the link that might explain how acres and acres of land zoned rural could be completely bulldozed and covered with buildings with nary a question asked. Even if Waters wouldn't talk just seeing what he looked like or where he lived might provide some clues that Tamara could run with.

After three days of searching there was nothing to be found. Not only was there no evidence that Jonas Waters ever received the sales proceeds, Tamara marveled, there was no evidence that he ever existed. Other than as documented in the auction records and land titles in question, Jonas Waters' name was absent from any public record to be found in Ogle County. Eventually, Tamara gave up and called Tom Sanders.

Tom was surprised to hear from her. "I was on the other side of the county and will be passing through your area in fifteen minutes," Tamara said. "Can I stop in?"

"Are you alone?"

"Yes, yes, of course. Why, is your house still under surveillance?"

"Not on a regular basis anymore. I was just curious whether you had anyone with you."

Tom couldn't explain why he hadn't expected to hear from Tamara. Perhaps because in the back of his mind he'd thought she was trying to lay low; too guilty to face him. Instead, however, she was at his doorstep within fifteen minutes just as she said.

"Are the ladies home?" she asked when Tom ushered her onto his den.

"No, they're out shopping. Shopping for Christmas already, believe it or not."

"Good. Not good, because I'd like to see them. But good, because I need to talk to you in private."

"Really?" Tom questioned, wondering and allowing his suspicions to take more hold than he thought right.

"Yes, because I can't find him anywhere."

"Who, Robert?"

"No, Jonas Waters. I've come to believe that he never existed."

Sanders remained silent until registering the name that Tamara was talking about. "His name was all over the auction records and land titles. Of course he existed. He's probably just moved far away from here by now."

"I'm not so sure. Other than the documents that you refer to there isn't any other public record of the man."

"How's that possible? There's a screening required when a person purchases a property at auction or, particularly, before land titles can be registered. If the records were bogus there would be an awful many people who knew about it."

"Maybe not if the right person was doing the orchestrating."

"Coulter?"

Tamara tilted her head to one shoulder and lifted her palms saying, without speaking, "It couldn't be anyone else."

Tom eyed Tamara cautiously. She came to visit anxious to tell him what she had found or, actually, couldn't find. Was she rallying the cause, seeking justice in the name of the LPS, or was she really working with Arthur Flemming just as Sonnvoldt had said and trying to lead him astray?"

"Why are you looking at me like that, Tom? Tell me what you make of this."

Tom recovered from his trance and answered, "I think we'll be working a long time before we'll be able to trace this back to Coulter."

"But what did you learn about the people who purchased the other properties?"

"I told you about Daniel Herbert. He was a real person."

"Sure he was but he's dead. What about the others?"

"I followed the transaction records, the land titles and so forth. That's when I pulled the council together to help color in the picture, which includes learning something about the backgrounds of the middlemen."

"Straw men, you mean? Let's talk to Andy and Jason to see what they've found out about the people involved in the transactions they were investigating. Maybe there's a broad pattern here."

Sanders curled his lips inward. After sufficient contemplation he said, "I'm sorry, Tamara, but before we discuss this matter any further we need to talk about something else."

"Okay, what?"

"Arthur Flemming. How involved are you?"

Tamara's face turned flush. "I don't know why it's so important to you, Tom. But if it makes you feel better; no, I'm not romantically involved with Arthur."

"It's important because you're a dear friend; however, I wasn't necessarily referring to your romantic involvement. I was referring more to your business relationship."

With only slight hesitation, Tamara replied, "It's the same as yours. We've agreed to be allies. So what are you trying to get at?"

Tom sighed. He didn't know how to respond until he remembered what he had told himself. "Be direct," he mumbled inaudibly.

"What?"

"Are you still with us or have you turned against the LPS?"

"What in the hell are you talking about, Tom?"

"I know it sounds crazy but Robert seems to believe that Flemming is using you and that possibly, knowingly or unknowingly, you're working with him."

"Robert? Is this why he didn't show up at our last meeting?"

"That might be part of it."

"I think he's gone off the deep end. And you, Tom, what about you? Why didn't you say something to me about this before?"

Tom was caught, ashamed of his mistrust yet wanting to press Tamara further for a direct response to his question. But he didn't need to press further. He knew her too well. Just by looking at her he knew that even the remotest possibility that she was working against the LPS was ludicrous. Nevertheless, there was one more matter involving Arthur Flemming that needed to be addressed.

"I'm sorry, Tamara, but it was all so shocking when Robert brought it up. Maybe I wasn't thinking straight either, especially after what I saw come up with Arthur's name on it."

"What was that?"

"There was another transaction that I didn't tell you about at the café. It was very similar to the others except that this time the developer turned out to be Arthur's company."

"But I didn't think Pinnacle was active in Ogle County."

"They really haven't been," Tom responded. "But they just so happened to take title to one of their only projects here via that mysterious zoning flip scenario."

Tamara sat stunned. Initially, before she decided to suggest that the LPS ally with him, she had been even more skeptical of Arthur Flemming than the rest of the group. She allowed herself to overcome her skepticism possibly in order to reconcile with the past. As a young adult she had a difficult time coming to grips with the fact that her parents were property developers. They were normal caring people. They weren't evil so how could they be property developers she often wondered. After many years in the business her parents also came to recognize the awful harm that over development raked on the landscape. They saw that enough was enough and changed their ways. Why not believe that Arthur Flemming could change as well? But had she allowed herself to be more than just willing to believe he could change? After some pondering, Tamara's stunned amazement gravitated toward an embarrassment of her own. Perhaps Robert saw something before she had. She had allowed Arthur to charm her: charm her so as to be able to manipulate her for his own ill intent.

# Chapter 23

As Carrie Anthony prepared to embark for Washington, D.C., in an attempt to unravel the chain of events that transformed Ogle County from a Semi-Rural designate to a self-ruled kingdom, Andy Cemanski was planning to visit the courthouse to uncover the missing man in a series of property transactions. Carrie never understood how Ogle County lost its Semi-Rural status and became a Mixed-Use designate in the first place. Wasn't there enough residential and commercial development in northern Illinois already? In fact, this question is what led to the formation of the Rural Reformers party and its members were still searching for answers nearly ten years later. And now the county administration was promoting development beyond the already liberal Mixed-Use expansion guidelines. Where were the checks and balances to assure compliance with federal regulations? Meanwhile, relative to another more specific situation, Andy couldn't believe that a fictitious name had been plastered onto multiple transfer agreements and land titles without a single person asking, "Who is that guy?"

Andy had copies of the bogus documents in his hand and was determined to find answers. He wanted to see the records proving that the proper authority had authenticated the buyer's signature. Andy decided to bypass the bureaucrats and go right to the Recorder of Deeds but security wouldn't allow him to pass that far. Andy was determined, however, and began questioning every official he saw demanding to know, "Who authorized these transactions?"

A commotion ensued and by the time Andy was escorted from the building he had created quite a scene. As armed guards grabbed him by each arm he flung the copies he carried up in the air. "Here," he screamed, "let the rest of the public get a look at this farce!"

Tom was furious when he heard what happened but tried calming down before meeting with Andy. We don't need two madmen on the council, he reckoned. "What were you thinking going off at the courthouse like that?" Tom asked.

"We've put up with this long enough, Tom; corrupt officials, corrupt deals. They think they own the whole county and they will if we don't stop them soon."

"If you could've just shown a little patience for once. Tamara had arrived at the same point as you had. The middleman for the property deals she was looking into appears to have been a figment of someone's imagination as well. We were practically on our way over to see you when I heard about the hubbub you'd raised."

"No kidding?"

"Right, no kidding. We've got a pattern here. We could be on the verge of exposing a huge scandal. But now, I just hope you haven't screwed the whole thing up. You've blown our cover before we've had the chance to dig up more details."

"I'm sorry, Tom, but I couldn't help myself. I've been living under that demigod's rule for too long."

"I understand, but we need to keep our heads. Let's keep real quiet for the next few weeks to make sure you haven't stirred up a bigger hornet's nest over at the county building than we might already think. In the meantime, why don't we see if Jason found out anything about the alleged farmer who bought the property he was investigating?"

"That's fine but there's still a few more possibilities I want follow-up on too."

"For God's sake, Andy. Hold off! You're not going to be any good to us if Coulter has you thrown in jail"

Tamara wheeled her vehicle up to express lane entrance, announced her exit ramp and was on her way to see Arthur Flemming. There would be no preliminaries; no waiting to read his reactions like Tom had waited for hers. She was going to come right out and ask what he was up to. She trembled envisioning the encounter, infuriated with Flemming but in truth angrier at allowing herself to be taken by his charm.

When Tamara arrived she was welcomed by Flemming's assistant and graciously escorted through the spacious living room, down a corridor to a den filled with memorabilia honoring the master's various achievements. As she waited, two plaques in particular caught Tamara's eye. The first engraving read, "Kane County Developer of the Year." The second read, "DeKalb's Finest Development." She shook her head and edged closer to study the underlying print but had little time before Arthur entered through a door at the opposite side of the room.

Arthur rushed across the floor and hugged her, exclaiming, "I was thrilled to hear that you were coming, Tamara. It's been way too long since our last visit. I can't wait to hear what you've been doing with yourself."

"Likewise," Tamara replied curtly as she took a step back.

"Let me have Donald bring us a glass of wine before we get started. I seem to recall your penchant for the Bordeaux that the French still think they're so damn good at fermenting. I believe there's one on the rack that we'll find to your taste."

"Never mind that, Arthur. Just tell me what in the hell you're up to!"

"I'm sorry. Did I say something to offend you?"

"Yes, you have offended me, by using me like you have so many others over your illustrious career."

"I hardly doubt that you'd give me the opportunity to use you, Ms. Hopkins. Please tell me what this is all about."

"You've manipulated me and you've used the LPS to gain a foothold in Ogle County. Why, Arthur, so that you can add to your trophy collection?" Tamara scoffed gesturing toward the plaques she'd observed earlier.

"I thought that we'd covered all of this already. I want to help you. What more can I tell you to demonstrate my sincerity?"

"What about the Native American burial grounds? Do you really give a damn about them or did you use that as a ploy, too, in order to distract Gardner while you swooped up more property on Prairie Parkway?"

"Well, Tamara, I'll admit that it would give me great pleasure to disrupt any plan of John Gardner's and I had considered that it'd be nice to give one of my managers a project to work on in Ogle County. But let me tell you that I've taken a great risk by planting the Indian burial ground rumor inside the ranks of the County Clerk's office. If Coulter found out that I was the one responsible for leaking that story, he'd see to it that I never stepped foot in his county again. As it were he was incensed by the idea that I might be working with you folks."

"So you admit to your motive to start more projects in Ogle County."

"Initially, that was part of it. Anyway, Pinnacle needs to make it look like we're getting something started in order to buy the LPS more time to increase your holdings and slow down other developers. Trust me though, any project we do start will be well-planned to minimize environmental impact."

"Trust you?"

"Yes. I know that's a lot to ask but at least give me a chance."

"You want me to trust a man who worked hand in glove with Coulter himself, devising a plan to create a mythical farmer to purchase rural lands so later they could be re-zoned for development purposes behind the public's back."

Flemming stared awkwardly at Tamara and began to speak but then hesitated. Before he could continue Tamara added, "Morgan Estates, Arthur. That's what I'm talking about."

Flemming looked down pinching his forehead with his thumb and forefinger. "That was a long time ago," he said softly.

"Can a man who freely participates in such deception ever change?"

"Maybe there was more to it than what you've been told."

"Like what? Anything that would make me feel differently than the way I feel right now?"

"Probably not but let me prove to you that I've changed."

For once Flemming seemed vulnerable but Tamara was determined to remain unmoved. She stared icily unconvinced that he was being completely honest. Finally she said, "Perhaps you can prove your sincerity for our cause. I want you to disclose everything you know about those land transactions. How did the whole scheme work? Name every single person who was involved."

"I suppose that I do owe you an explanation, Tamara."

"You owe more than just me. I want you to take this story to the press. Blow the lid off of this scandal."

Flemming rubbed his upper lip thoughtfully. "I can't," he said.

"You can't, or you won't?"

"Please understand that despite our large estates, people like myself and John Gardner are merely vassals. Nathan Coulter is the king of Ogle County and, whether it be the eleventh century or today, the king expects his vassals to comply with his rules. The king has ways of controlling the lords of his properties and has harsh penalties for those who cross the line."

"Didn't you cross the line when you stirred up the burial ground information?"

"That'll invite his wrath if discovered but it doesn't involve a specific property, say Morgan Estates, to which he entrusted me as his vassal."

"Rather a conflict wouldn't you say to desire to be entrusted by both Nathan Coulter and the LPS?" Tamara stated harshly yet somehow sympathetic as if knowing that the great businessman's empire was about to be destroyed. "Woe is the man who serves two masters."

"Look, Tamara, I want to be as much help to you as I can but let's leave the Morgan Estates issue alone for now. The approach we're taking with the Indian burial grounds and the other properties we have will help build a solid base."

"Those strategies are only temporary stops. We need to change the entire regime in Ogle County."

"All in good time."

"We're running out of time, Arthur. If you'd please have Donald retrieve my wrap, I'll be moving along now."

"Let's talk this through, Tamara."

"Until you're ready to prove yourself I don't need to hear anymore," Tamara sneered and turned to leave the den in search of Donald and her overcoat.

# Chapter 24

The holidays were past and the council was at a crossroads. When they acquired the auctioned properties back in the summer they were optimistic yet unsure of how they'd leverage their gains for the good of the LPS. Now they were more uncertain than ever. Robert Sonnvoldt still refused to rejoin the council and was bargaining to assume sole control over the land in the northwest sector. Their alliance with Arthur Flemming appeared finished and, then, so did the help they'd need to expand their holdings in the more expensive central region of the county.

When the professor uncovered suspicious zoning changes the council thought that they were on to something big. The subsequent discovery that fictitious individuals had been concocted to facilitate the shady deals offered the promising possibility that Nathan Coulter's dark side could be revealed for all to see. However, the council had been forced to proceed more cautiously than ever after Andy's tirade at the courthouse. The incident made news and not necessarily in a light sympathetic to the point Andy was trying to make. Now they were at dead ends until they could find the "smoking gun" that proved Coulter or one of his henchmen had approved the deals.

"After the negative publicity you received," Tom said in Andy's direction, "it'd be risky to take the story to the press prematurely."

"Let's flush out Flemming then and make him spill the beans," Andy suggested. "Sounds like he's already implicated Coulter from what Tamara told us."

The rest of the council rejected Andy's idea noting that they didn't trust Flemming but reasoning that he was no more on Coulter or Gardner's side than they were. Arthur might not be with the LPS; however, for the time being, he provided somewhat of a neutralizing influence. Pushing him too far, they feared, might cause Flemming to gravitate toward the corner of their primary nemeses.

"Why don't we let somebody else fight our battles?" Jason McAlpin eventually offered as the council struggled to determine their next move. "We can put all our resources behind the Rural Reformers and let them do the dirty work."

"The easy way always seems more appealing," Tom countered, "but in the long-run that strategy might end all hope. The chances that the Rural Reformers win the election are still remote. By the end of April they might be nothing more than a historical footnote and then where will we be?" Tom paused briefly before answering his own question. "I'd rather not think about that, so instead of waiting, we need to pursue the initiatives we've already established to assure that at least one platform remains in the fight for land preservation."

"I appreciate your spirit, professor. However, we can hardly afford to buy more land and you don't want me poking around to dig up more dirt on those phony transactions, so just which initiatives are you suggesting that we pursue?" Andy asked unapologetically.

"Well, Flemming may no longer be working with us but that doesn't mean we can't run with the bone he threw us. I say we get back on track toward finding out more about the burial grounds. Perhaps we can get an injunction thrown on Gardner's development and at the same time see if Mr. Coulter flinches under public scrutiny."

"I agree," Tamara chimed. "Given the professor's acumen for historical research we ought, pardon the pun, be able to dig up a few skeletons."

"Whoa!" Andy exclaimed. "You're the one who normally points out the risks, professor, but I think I'd be remiss not to remind you that it was our poking into Gardner's property that almost got you killed."

"Point considered; however, I feel good enough about this hunch to be willing to face that danger again. If you're behind me on this, that is."

Andy folded his burly arms and stated, "You don't have to ask twice. I'm with you, professor."

Jason contemplated what had been decided and commented, not completely in jest, "Does this mean we're off to dig up Chief Black Hawk?"

"No, Jason. As I said before, these burial grounds date to an era many moons before the coming of Black Hawk."

# Chapter 25

Walking over hallowed ground and surveying the landscape in person would instill vivid mental images that would prove invaluable later, bringing life to the subject when studied in text. This was Tom's intent when he suggested a trip the next morning, "to sojourn the haunts of our American fore bearers." He felt that witnessing the burial site, whether or not truly discernible, would provide added motivation to begin his research in earnest. Tamara didn't argue for she was also interested in observing the property.

Tom was eager, practically waiting on the doorstep, when Tamara arrived to pick him up that morning. He pointed her in the right direction and they were quickly on their way. "I hope we're not arrested for trespassing," Tamara told him as they drove to the site.

"Don't worry it's too cold this time of year for any of Gardner's folks to be out at the property. They're all holed up in their offices reviewing visuals and maps."

"Oh, great! I just thought of something else," Tamara exclaimed.

"What is it?"

"We're in my vehicle. If anybody spots it on the grounds they'll be able to trace it back to me."

"Better you than me," Tom responded.

"Fine friend you are."

"I'm just kidding. You raise a good point. When we get closer, we'll pull over and take your tags off."

After crossing the Rock River they continued southwest on a narrow country highway heading into a sector of the county remarkably unscathed by major development. Tom's trained eyes noticed the change in terrain as they proceeded. They entered an increasingly hilly area containing gentle valleys where streams ran, which provided a marked contrast to the otherwise flat regional topography. As they traveled further the road seemed to rise above the landscape and Tom breathed in the vastness of the surrounding vista from his passenger seat perch. "You can see for miles. The sky just seems bigger out here," he exalted. "Remind me to come back in the spring when the grass is green and the trees begin to bloom."

When they drew within a mile of their destination Tom directed Tamara to a gravel drive near what appeared to be an abandoned farmhouse. Here they removed the tags from Tamara's vehicle and placed them under the front seat before continuing on to Gardner's property, formerly known as Meador Farms. The land had been in the Meador family for well over a century before finally succumbing to the auction block. Never used as cropland, the property remained quite rustic. The open expanses nestled between wooded hills and marshy lowlands were better suited for pasture so, alternately over the years, the acreage was used to train horses or raise sheep.

"Are you sure we're still in Ogle County?" Tamara remarked as she slowed to almost a stop in front of the property.

"I'm sure," Tom answered. "Kind of makes you realize there's a lot of beautiful land that's worth saving, doesn't it?"

"Sure does."

Tamara found the main entrance to the old Meador homestead, turned in and drove up the lane until her vehicle was comfortably out of sight from the public roadway. There didn't appear to be anyone around. However, as he exited the vehicle, Tom noticed the familiar stakes used by surveyors planted to the right of the family home. They outlined the first stage of Gardner's planned development. "Already?" Tom mumbled as he stepped forward.

Tamara stepped around the front of the vehicle stopping next to Tom while drawing the strings of her overcoat tighter. The air was crisp as would be expected for January but not Arctic. The sun was shining and the ground dry with only a few patches of snow remnant from the last storm well over a week ago. Conditions were ideal for a winter hike.

"Which way do we go, professor?"

"Your guess is as good as mine."

"I'd go that way," said Tamara pointing beyond the house to the left in a southwesterly direction.

"How come?"

"The elevation appears to rise toward that way and there, off past those trees, I see a ridgeline. There'll be a panoramic view of this entire property up on top, I'm sure. That's where I'd want to be buried if I'd have lived on these lands."

"Seems logical."

"Of course it is. Let's go," Tamara retorted proudly. She was partly poking fun at Tom, letting him know she'd trumped him at his game, but also eager to keep moving to ward off the chill.

Beyond a stable, they followed a dirt lane lined by maple trees on one side and a wooden rail fence on the other. The fence bordered a pasture well suited for horses to graze. There had been none there, however, not since the last of the Meador line abandoned the property two years before. That Meador wanted to pass title to a family friend but couldn't wait for financing to be arranged as his own debts piled higher. That's when the land went to auction and Gardner swooped in recognizing the potential of the large tract and understanding that the march of development in the county would eventually head this direction.

Where the fence line took a right angle and the dirt lane followed, Tom and Tamara chose the footpath that continued forward and led down to a meadow and over a partially frozen brook. On the other side, the path began to rise to the ridge that Tamara had pointed to earlier. The hillside was dotted with majestic hardwoods spaced far enough apart to have allowed sheep to forage on lazy summer afternoons.

"Isn't this that pastoral setting they show in cinema to create the sense that you're stepping back into a gentler era. You know the scene, 'Man returns to boyhood home'."

"Yeah, I think you've captured the feeling, Tam," Tom responded as he scanned the hillside.

In another five minutes they reached the top of the ridge. Tamara had assumed correctly. The position provided a far-reaching view. The pastures were below, beyond the brook, and the Meador home stood in the distance. Off to the other side, a forested slope gave way to farm lots segregated by hedgerows and tree lines. Further out, the spires of two churches rose above the horizon to frame the edges of a tiny village. Swept up by the beauty of the area, Tom and Tamara almost forgot their mission. But then Tom refocused to the closer surrounds of the ridge top looking for more subtle elevation changes, ditches, mounds: contours in the land created by humans. The professor walked slowly now rummaging for clues to a lost civilization. He wasn't searching for signs of the earliest Meador but rather for a community prospering possibly thousands of years previously.

Tamara broke his concentration by quipping, "Wouldn't you think there'd be a marker saying here lies … I mean, come on, it's not like we're the first ones to ever scale this summit. Surely Grandpa Meador brought his grandkids up here and told stories about the great herds of buffalo while they all sat around the chief's grave."

"Not necessarily. You see, some archaeologist somewhere else may have found something just a few years ago that somehow made reference to this particular hill that had been otherwise previously overlooked."

"Boy, if that didn't sound like an answer from a professor I don't know ..."

"No seriously, Tam. Another possibility is that when the surveyors came out here to map this property before it went to auction last summer they may have dug in an area that hadn't been overturned since pre-recorded history. They may have discovered bones or relics."

"Well if that's the case, I'm sure either Coulter's aides or John Gardner, whoever found out first, instructed them to cover everything over before anyone else could see them."

"Unfortunately, you're probably right."

They sleuthed around the hilltop for another half an hour before Tamara said that she had, "better get back to keep her afternoon appointments." Tom agreed that he wouldn't find much more that day so they headed back to Tamara's vehicle. Despite having no more hard evidence than when they arrived, the professor was content in knowing that he had gained an understanding of the lay of the land that would prove useful to his subsequent research.

Tamara's vehicle was near the house where they had left it ostensibly unseen. Even if Gardner's employees had happened across it they'd have had a hard time requesting an ownership search considering that the auto was a common make stripped of its identifying markers. However, there was a man who saw them, peering at them from behind a shade in the vacated residence as they returned from their hike. His steely stare followed them as they drove away and turned back onto the country highway.

They didn't realize they'd been watched and rode in quiet contentment until after several miles when the land began to flatten Tom turned to Tamara and said, "I came, today, to be inspired by the sanctity of those grounds. I can't say I felt the aura from the burial site that I'd anticipated but, nonetheless, the simple beauty of the land moved me. With or without historical significance, I think it's worth fighting to save."

"I don't think there's a member of the LPS who'd argue and, hopefully, there are many more citizens who feel the same way."

Tamara dropped Tom off at his house and continued to her office where she worked late into the evening to make up for the time she'd lost that morning. It was past eleven p.m. by the time she arrived home and when she turned into her driveway her headlights illuminated a piece of paper that had been affixed to the front door. She stopped before entering the garage to retrieve the paper, unfolding it to read a note that had been neatly imprinted by hand. The inscription read, "Tamara, your face is so pretty. It would be a shame to see it mangled because you were sticking your nose where it didn't belong."

# Chapter 26

Tamara waved her palm over the sensor and fumbled with the knob frantically until it released. Barely through the threshold, she slammed the door shut and bolted the lock all in one motion. That accomplished, she let her backside fall against the doorjamb while exhaling and closing her eyes. But they quickly reopened and scanned the room. Had anyone broken in? A locked door didn't stop the intruder at Tom and Tamara's house.

She grabbed her largest kitchen knife and began a slow, methodical search through her town home. She held the weapon pointed down, close against her leg, in a position where she hoped it couldn't be turned against her in the event she was jumped from behind. After a thorough inspection of every potential hiding place and noting nothing in disarray, she convinced herself that her security system had not been breached. However, she did notice that her face was drenched in perspiration. *Maybe today's walk and this adrenaline rush will compensate for the lack of exercise I've been getting the last few weeks,* she kidded herself trying to bring levity to her frightened condition.

Trying to sleep proved fruitless and so, despite the late hour, she decided to call Tom. "Are you still up?"

"Well, yeah, sort of."

"They saw us at Meador Farms."

"What? Who?"

Tamara explained what she had found on her door and read the ominous message back to Tom.

"I'll be right over!"

"No, I'm fine. I have a very good security system here, so this problem can wait until morning. Remember that you have a wife and daughter to take care of."

"Are you sure you're all right?"

"Yes. We can talk tomorrow."

"If you don't want to talk tonight, then why did you call? So I can worry all night too?"

"Well yeah, sort of."

The next morning, after escorting Colleen to school, Tom took Marina with him to see Tamara. They weren't dealing with just an LPS matter any longer. This concerned the safety and well being of all of them and likely several others as well. Tamara had remained brave staying alone at her town home through the night but tears began to well as much in relief as anything else when she saw her friends on the front step. She handed Tom the note to read first after the trio had taken a seat in the kitchen. He chewed his lower lip at a loss for words before passing the slip of paper along to his wife. Marina quivered as she read, beginning to feel that same sense of fear that had enveloped her entire being for those few days after her own home had been invaded.

Marina's anxiety was quickly tempered by outrage. Still frustrated by the lack of information the police had compiled on her husband's assailant she offered to, "deliver the note directly to Coulter's grubby hands. These blatant acts of intimidation are obviously related. Coulter was elected to protect the citizenry and maintain order in this county so he'd better start having his law enforcement officers connect the dots on these crimes."

"Coulter? You think he gives a damn about protecting us?" Tom responded finally able to speak.

"Maybe not but there must be a few within his ranks who still feel obligated to uphold peace and justice."

The three of them came to the understanding that the handwritten threat had to be brought in for investigation. "She shouldn't go by herself though. She should have a legal representative," Marina advised, "but not me." Tom and Tamara agreed. Marina was too personally involved to be effective counsel. However, as someone who'd make a worthy substitute and as someone she knew could not turn down the assignment, Marina volunteered her trusted associate to accompany Tamara to police headquarters. "My associate has a few connections and she'll make sure that someone high up in the organization is aware of the matter and takes it seriously."

"The question is," stated Tom, "are we ready to suggest that this vicious threat is related to the break-in at our house? That will unquestionably link Tamara and I together and draw attention to the LPS."

"I think we have to. This is getting too dangerous."

"Marina's right," Tamara interjected. "Besides, at this point, a little publicity might be good for us. How can Coulter worry about restraining the LPS while his police chief is dealing with unsolved crimes and violent criminals are on the loose? The public is certain to think his priorities are out of whack if he does."

Later that day when Andy found out about the note left on Tamara's door he was beside himself and immediately on his way to see her. "Are you sure that you're okay staying here by yourself, sweetie?"

"Yes. I've told you guys that I have a very good security system."

"We're dealing with ruthless individuals here."

"I can take care of myself, Andy."

"You'll promise to let me know if you need help though."

"I will."

"Okay," Andy said looking into her eyes and pausing before continuing. "You know I came over here because I'm concerned about you, Tamara, but there was something else I was getting ready to call you about anyway. I've been looking into the straw man that purchased the large farm now known only as Western Landings."

"Andrew, I thought we all agreed to put those investigations on hold for now."

"I know but I had a lead I couldn't let pass. Besides, at this point, investigating Western Landings certainly doesn't appear to be anymore dangerous than poking into those burial grounds."

Tamara rolled her eyes acknowledging Andy's point. "Okay but what have you told Tom about this?"

"Nothing. Until he clearly sees where I'm going with this he wouldn't understand. He has his ways of gathering information and I have mine."

"Tell me what you're up to."

"There's a recording agent over at the county courthouse. She's there at every auction, inconspicuously going about her work. Well, I've gotten to know her over the years. Nice lady, even if she does work for the County Clerk's office. Turns out she was able to call up the photo of the gent who purchased the property. There's a camera system in the building that routinely takes a shot of anyone that places a bid. I'm sure they have your face on record there too. Anyway, after my friend studies the picture she recognizes the man. She thinks he was this unassuming fellow who used to work in another one of Coulter's departments. At this point, she told me she didn't want to get any further involved but after a little sweet-talking I convinced her to give me the name matching the photo. Armed with that, I was able to track him down."

Tamara's green eyes widened and she leaned forward. "Was he willing to talk to you?"

"Not really but he will."

"Andrew, you're awful. That sounds like something John Gardner would say."

"Sorry, I didn't mean it like that. I'm not going to force information out of him. I'm just gonna watch him for a while; figure out what he likes and what he doesn't. See where he goes. This guy might provide the key to breaking our case wide open."

# Chapter 27

Three days in a row the professor cleared his afternoon schedule to devote himself solely to research. Twice he finished morning lectures and on the third day he participated in a half-day symposium before returning to his University office where he'd spent hours without achieving any result. The professor was too worked up over the message left at Tamara's home to garner the concentration necessary for the meticulous task of poring through academic journals. Normally Tom would find reading studies on Native American tribes that prospered hundreds or thousands of years ago fascinating; however, not so much now under current circumstances.

Tom's strength resided in his ability to channel energy into logic, which was often used to piece together common threads of information that were otherwise disparate to the ordinary observer. In this case, the intended fruit of his labor would be the presentation of a well-developed argument that appealed to public emotion and effectively converted his logic into their energy. His adversaries utilized a less fine-tuned mental approach, more physical and, if not ultimately as effective, quicker at yielding results to foil their opposition. Their brazen intimidation was meant to disrupt the LPS's flow of energy causing it to be manifested in anxiety rather than logic.

On the fourth day, the professor found resolve by conjuring images of the council's adopted hero. Black Hawk fought back against the usurpation of free lands; however, upon detailed analysis he made somewhat of an ironic icon for the group. Previous to his valiant stand it was Black Hawk's people, the Sac and Fox, who essentially drove the Illinois tribes off lands that they had inhabited for hundreds upon hundreds of years.

Now, Tom clutched for a comment made by Arthur Flemming when he first told them about the Native American burial site on Gardner's property. "I believe they may have been migrants of the Mississippians." The professor remembered the words clearly because he was amazed at the time that a non-academician, a cunning man no less that seemed solely focused on business, had even heard of this ancient tribe.

"The site dates back something like fifteen hundred to two thousand years," Flemming had declared. History on the Illinois tribes going that far back is not clear, which made it more likely that a settlement from that period was indeed from a people that had traveled up the Mississippi River valley from the south. Later in their first conversation, Flemming was obviously trying to impress upon Tom's academic credentials. "They were said to be mound builders you know."

The latter comment didn't really make sense. There was no evidence of mounds in the area. There were further south, in Cahokia, Illinois, where one of the continent's most well documented mound sites existed. The Cahokia tribe's culture and economic center flourished there sometime between 700 and 1400 A.D.

Flemming's reference to the mounds may have been misplaced but it didn't discredit his overall claim. The Mississippians were known to trade and travel prior to their more industrious era, which is the timeframe to which Flemming initially pointed. So with no mound cities in existence yet, why wouldn't a community settle near a geological ridgeline in southwestern Ogle County, atop fertile soil and abundant hunting grounds and in close proximity to the Rock River?

Everything Flemming said lined up. Nothing contradicted the scholarly notes Sanders read concerning the general history of Native Americans in the area. On the other hand though, there was nothing he could find to corroborate Flemming's specific assertion either. Still there were more volumes to be reviewed. Nevertheless, the professor couldn't help but think a commissioned archaeological dig might get him to the bottom of this mystery a lot faster. But that wasn't going to happen. What was he supposed to do, ask Gardner or Coulter for permission to dig? Besides, disturbing the remains of the ancients may infuriate a certain portion of the constituency he was attempting to rally to his cause.

# Chapter 28

Arthur Flemming called three times but Tamara refused to pick up. Finally, he left a message. "I heard about the threat you received. I want to help you."

Tamara read the text message wondering how Flemming had found out about the note. She speculated on the nature of the help he had in mind but chose not to inquire. Instead, she decided to call Andy Cemanski. Tamara thought of Andy fondly, like a father figure or maybe more like a well-meaning impetuous uncle. She was worried that he'd go off stirring up more trouble than he could handle. Andy was determined to unravel the mystery behind the shady land deals and she knew his inclination to press matters to the limit.

In some respects she'd wished Andy had never told her about what he had found. She wanted to tell Tom and Jason so that all would be in on it together but unfortunately Andy would confide only in her. He knew Tom would try to talk him out of trailing the straw man. She couldn't violate Andy's trust but she figured that she better keep her eye on him. "I'm going to find out what that stubborn old man is up to," Tamara mumbled to herself as she picked up her communication device.

Andy didn't respond when she called. He had turned off all electronic devices as he followed at a safe distance behind the straw man. The previous week, Cemanski finally met his straw man in person and eventually the man grew more comfortable with Andy and opened up. As the man talked Andy learned that he was very bitter. His role in the dubious Western Landings transaction wasn't as rewarding as he had expected. After witnessing the lavish lifestyles of the developers and certain of the higher-ups at the County Clerk's office, the man had begun to have second thoughts about the equity of his pay out.

"I gave up a promising government career and have been forced to keep a low profile for what? I received a hundred thousand bucks give or take. But ask me how much of that's left. I got nothing, man."

As Andy looked around the shabby little home he had to agree and the more they talked the more he felt that the man was ripe for coughing up his sources. His allegiance had dissolved and the perceived retribution he'd receive for squealing had diminished over the years.

"Where are the records that show how the land got re-zoned from rural to unrestricted residential and commercial?" Andy prodded.

"I don't know. I don't think they wanted me to be involved with any of that and, frankly, I didn't want to be involved."

"I see," Andy sighed and then redirected his questions. He asked more about the man's background trying to show an interest in him personally. He was exercising patience, not looking over-anxious, which wasn't easy for Andy to do. Eventually he returned to his objective.

"Who provided you with the money to fund the land purchase?"

"I'm not allowed to ask his name but I still see him once a month."

Andy almost choked as he considered the potential opportunity. "You're kidding?"

"No. I have to collect my allowance. They didn't want me to get everything up front, you see. They want to be able to keep in touch with me."

"That seems unusual," Cemanski commented attempting to regain his composure.

"Yeah, I used to think so too but I guess I've gotten used to it. As a matter of fact, I go pick up my allowance tomorrow."

"Really," Andy responded placing his hand to his forehead. He hesitated and then asked, "Say, would you mind if I came with you tomorrow and took a look at this fellow?"

"Hmm, I don't think you should come with me but if you'd like to follow without being noticed that'd probably be okay. Be careful though because they've warned me about trying any funny business."

So now, here Andy found himself following the straw man as he traveled to meet his benefactor. They were heading to a nature preserve, which Andy considered ironic yet to his advantage. He was very familiar with the preserve and based upon the precise meeting place the straw man described just before they started their journey, Andy determined the perfect observation point from where he'd be out of sight.

When the straw man turned into the nature preserve and veered to the right at a fork in the road, Andy went to the left. Andy continued around the looping road until reaching nearly the furthest point from the preserve's entrance. There, he parked in a small gravel lot, exited his vehicle and ascended a modest slope. His path led him through a forest that, despite stark winter conditions, he felt provided ample cover for his clandestine operation. At the apex of the backside of the hill he found a vantage point overlooking the preserve's main parking area. Being the dead of winter, the lot was empty except for the straw man's automobile parked off to one side. Within minutes a limousine rolled into the lot and came to a stop next to the straw man. Cemanski trained his binoculars intently on the larger vehicle anxious to see who might step out. He waited for what seemed an eternity and nothing happened. "Come on," he whispered, "come out of your chariot and show me who you are."

Then, Andy shivered. It wasn't from the cold but rather from an eerie sensation that penetrated his body. He suddenly felt as if he was being watched; where he was vulnerable, alone on the hillside. He slowly turned his head and then his shoulders followed until he could see what was behind him. The barrel of a pistol was directed straight at his head.

"Hello, Mr. Cemanski. Mr. Bass would like to have a word with you."

With that said, the man motioned with his weapon to indicate that Andy should begin walking down the slope to the lot where the straw man and the limousine were parked. While they descended, with the gunman in the rear, the straw man drove away. "Shit," Andy exhaled quietly. Then, as they neared the remaining vehicle, Andy recognized the man behind the wheel. It was Collin Bass, indistinguishable to most but not to Andy. Bass was Nathan Coulter's top political aide and arguably the second most powerful man in the county. The aide held a non-elected post and steered clear of the limelight yet wielded influence over most county matters.

Bass lowered his window and called, "Greetings, Andy. I'm glad you were able to make it out here today on such short notice. But then, I had no doubt that you'd show. You're so charmingly predictable."

"So this was all a set-up?"

"I'd rather refer to this as an appointment."

"Bull shit! That's just another one of the phony aphorisms you use to sugar coat your lies."

"Oh, Andy, I've really missed our chats. You know, if the size of your brain was anywhere near the size of your heart maybe you'd have been working with us for all of these years."

"What do you want from me, Mr. Bass?"

"I've just a few questions. For starters, who's working with you on this little assignment of yours?"

"I only work solo."

"Of course you do. What's your relationship with Arthur Flemming?"

"There is none."

"Are you working with the Rural Reformers?"

"In case you forgot, I'll remind you that your boss banned me from all political activity."

"All right then, I don't have any more questions. You see, Andy, that wasn't too bad," Bass concluded and then raised his window.

Before he drove away, Bass motioned to the gunman by lifting two fingers and then pulling them down and over across his neck. The gunman instantly fired a round into Andy's forehead and the impact drove his body sprawling backward across the pavement. He raised his left knee, instinctively, ready to spring up for a fight. But the reaction was fleeting and Andy was dead.

# Chapter 29

She pounded furiously on the front door without response before scurrying around the side of the house. She rapped as hard she could on what she thought was his bedroom window and still nothing. The hour was approaching midnight and Tamara had become frantic after trying to reach him for the last two days. Andy was known to completely engross himself in whatever activity was currently atop his agenda but surely he would have checked in by now. If he was trailing a hot lead he'd be too excited not to call, she insisted.

"I can't find him!"

Oh boy, Tom thought as he roused himself from bed, what now? "Are you all right?"

"I'm fine but I can't find him."

"Who is it?" Marina asked as she rolled over.

"Tamara."

"Oh, my God, is she okay?"

"She says she's fine." Then Tom spoke back into the direct link, "Who are you looking for?"

"Andy. I was just at his house and he wasn't there."

"Maybe he's at his girlfriend's house. Yeah, I bet that's it. Call Minnie," Tom suggested not yet comprehending the gravity of the situation.

"Who?"

"You know, the waitress at the café."

"Damn it, Tom! I'm serious. There's something going on. I've been calling him for two days and he hasn't picked up."

"I'm sorry, I'm tired. Please start from the beginning."

Tamara began by telling him about Andy's visit the previous week. "He said he found the straw man in the Western Landings deal."

Tom felt his throat constrict as Tamara relayed her conversation with Andy. He began to fear the worst. Had Andy pushed Gardner too far? Then guilt took over. *I should have heard him out and been there to work with him on this case,* Tom lamented. While Tamara continued with her story, Tom felt like screaming to suppress all feelings of guilt and anxiety. *I told him to leave Western Landings alone* he wanted to say. But he fought the urge recognizing the internal process of cognitive dissonance working to blame his friend for his own demise.

As Tamara finished her account Sanders tried to settle his nerves. He struggled to ask calmly, "Can we find this straw man? Perhaps he can lead us to Andy."

"Andy never told me his name. But wait, yes, maybe we can go back to the woman at the courthouse who showed Andy the picture."

The county courthouse opened at nine a.m. and Tom and Tamara were already inside searching for Andy's confidante. Two male employees and a lady too young to meet Andy's description were idly chatting in the area Tamara recollected from her conversation. When one of the men stepped aside Tom approached him and asked, "Isn't there an older woman who works in your department?"

"You mean Mrs. Mraz?"

"Yeah, that's right" Tom responded playing the chance that this was the correct name.

"Friday was her last day. She just came in and told us she was retiring."

This wasn't the answer he was expecting; however, Tamara was ready to step in to help. "Do you know how we can get in touch with her?"

"Nope. She said she'd had it with cold weather and was on her way to Arizona."

"Who were her friends here? Maybe they could help us?" Tamara suggested.

"I don't know. Why don't you try asking up at the information desk?"

Sanders glanced at Tamara with concern, thinking how odd it was that the woman just happened to retire the previous week and that her former co-worker, in a small department, knew relatively nothing about her. Then, almost simultaneously, they each experienced the eerie sensation that they were being watched. Before they could turn back to thank the man for his time he was gone.

"Let's get out of here,"

They exited the courthouse and hurried across the street deciding in route to stop at the Greenery Restaurant to discuss their next step over a cup of coffee. Their first thought was to file a missing person report but quickly determined that it would be fruitless. It was unlikely they'd get much sympathy at police headquarters in their search for Andy Cemanski. Somehow they'd have to find the trail of the straw man just as Andy had.

As their waitress refreshed their coffee cups Tom received a message on his direct link. It was Marina her voice was shaky. "You haven't seen the news?"

"No."

"Andy's dead."

"My God!"

Tom raced to the front counter, grabbed the local news source and brought it back to the table where he and Tamara read together, "A local man was found dead in his automobile at an Ogle County nature preserve. Andrew J. Cemanski, age 68, shot himself once in the head and likely died instantly. A preserve superintendent discovered Cemanski's body upon investigating the vehicle, which he had noticed parked in the same location the previous day."

Their worst fear was confirmed. Tom closed his eyes as his head tilted downward while Tamara began sobbing uncontrollably. He put his arm around her and she buried her head in his chest where it remained for several minutes. The waitress saw their anguish and was afraid to get close enough to the table to deliver the bill. So Tom finally swept his payment card through the transaction reader and they slowly exited the restaurant.

The funeral that followed was heartfelt and well attended. Other than his son and daughter's family Andy didn't have many relatives and, what he told Collin Bass moments before his death was largely true, he normally did work alone. However, the crusty warrior made many friends over his lifetime. His opposition loathed him but those who needed help knew that there was no one quicker to lend a hand. His friends might not have always understood his means but they admired his passion. Carrie Anthony was at the funeral and, surprisingly, so was Arthur Flemming.

# Chapter 30

The remaining three continued mourning their fallen friend and fellow council member and pondered their future without him. Formulating strategy proved difficult as each of them, alternately, offered an additional tribute. Jason McAlpin summed up his final homage by declaring, "Our modern day Black Hawk has been vanquished." His statement rang in the realization that with Andy gone so might go the rest of the council. With more than one opening the by laws prescribed that the LPS membership was required to hold an election for not just the vacated seats but for the entire council. Given the recent turmoil anything was bound to happen. Potentially, there was a block of members who'd see fit to move in a different direction and who'd lobby to find a replacement for each seat. The incumbents were torn as to how they wanted to see the election go. Drained, each of them was ready to accept removal yet; on the other hand, they felt compelled to complete their mission. Tamara and Jason were looking to Tom for direction. Could he still rally their cause, perhaps by presenting stirring findings concerning the sacred Indian burial site?

"Frankly, I haven't found a lick of concrete evidence," the professor stated. "Like everything else we've pursued the matter is laden with uncertainty. But in the meantime, an unrelenting onslaught of senseless development continues to ravage our county. Every sector is vulnerable now. So this is it, we can't wait any longer. Ready or not I'm going before the membership to tell them that Meador Farms is where we make our stand."

"Will you present any other options?"

"No. We need to maintain a focus," Sanders stated conclusively. After a brief pause he began to elaborate the details of the speech he intended to present regarding the Indian burial ground rumor and the Meador Farms property. He'd been captivated by the pastoral setting on which the alleged cemetery for the ancients resided ever since his hike on that crisp January morning. He may not have fully comprehended it at the time but it was then that he resolved that Meador Farms would become the LPS rallying cry.

As Tom continued to lay out what he'd say his passion erupted and his words became more eloquent. Then, as if the spirit of Andy Cemanski had carried upon the wind and entered through his pores, Sanders grew animated. First Tamara and then Jason recognized the possibilities behind this powerful medium. The gifted intellect of the professor had merged with a fervent emotion capable of transcending the malaise of the masses and delivering them to reason. Under his direction, thousands who'd unwittingly acquiesced to the actions of a relative few might yet unite to put a stop to the relentless destruction of land.

As they departed that evening, Tom felt flush. There was an aura about him and he was well aware that he'd moved his associates. But, alas, he was an ordinary man cognizant of his limitations and doubtful that he'd be capable of willing the populace to take action.

Flemming didn't bother to call this time. Instead, he paid a personal visit to Tamara's office.

"Ms. Hopkins, there is a Mr. Arthur Flemming here to see you," her assistant announced. "I didn't see where he has an appointment but he insisted that you be made aware that he's waiting."

Tamara gathered herself. Okay, why not see what he wants so that he'll stop calling she thought. "Show him in," she instructed her assistant.

Flemming was dressed more casually than was normal for him and he seemed to be in a stoical mood. When Tamara's aide closed the door upon leaving the office he began with condolences. "I'm extremely sorry about the tragedy that befell Andy Cemanski. I know that his passing must have been very difficult on you, personally, as well as on the entire LPS organization."

"I appreciate your sympathies."

"I still can't believe that…"

"Stop right there," Tamara interrupted. "Andy Cemanski did not kill himself. That man never gave up on anything and he wasn't about to give up on his own life. Andy Cemanski was murdered!"

"I'm sorry, Tamara, but I wasn't about to suggest that he did kill himself. I was going to say that I still couldn't believe that Coulter's gone this far. After I learned that his people left that note on your door I really wanted to get in touch with you and, then, when I heard about Cemanski…"

Tamara wrinkled her nose and squinted one eye, she looked confused but Arthur continued. "Anyway, when I heard they'd threatened you it really gave me second thoughts about the conversation we'd had a few weeks before. You were right. I need to blow the lid off his fixes and phony transactions because, apparently, the man will stop at nothing."

"Wait, back up," Tamara requested. "I thought it was John Gardner's people who left that note."

"Gardner may be a ruthless businessman but I don't think he's quite into that type of activity. Coulter, on the other hand, has been absolutely corrupted by power, which he seeks to make more absolute as each day passes. He will justify any means to maintain the balance of order in his county."

"Did he murder Andy?"

"I doubt that Andy's killer will ever be apprehended but you can be sure that Coulter was the one who ultimately issued the command."

Tamara took a deep breath as she fought back the tears she felt begin to well. "So now you're willing to do whatever it takes to expose this criminal?"

"It's risky and I don't know if it will be enough to bring him down but I can shed light on how he was able to maneuver the zoning changes on the properties your good friend, the professor, stumbled upon. Furthermore, I'm intimately familiar with certain other illegal activities that took place prior to that."

"Who are you going to take your story to: the Feds, the press?"

"Probably both in order to increase the odds that someone listens. You never know who Coulter's already reached."

"Why haven't you gone to them already? Why are you telling me first?"

"I don't know for sure myself. I think it might be that I'm trying to reconcile my guilt. When I saw you again after all those years I'd hoped that we'd be able to establish a relationship and I recognize that the reason we haven't is my fault. I wasn't completely honest with you at the outset. So now I want to demonstrate that I'm sincere and that I finally understand what you've been fighting for."

Flemming stopped speaking for a moment as he studied Tamara trying to discern the impact of his statement. Tamara was cool. She'd settled the emotions he'd stirred when he informed her that Coulter was responsible for Andy's murder. "You know, Tamara," Flemming began again, "there's a new element of danger you'll face if I tell you the details of my story. If Coulter finds out that you know what I know he may go beyond simply leaving notes on your doorstep. If you'd prefer, perhaps I shouldn't tell you anything more."

"I suppose I understand the risk but I need to know. If you don't tell me and you were to meet an unfortunate end then ... well, you know, we need to increase the odds that someone tells your story? So please, go on and tell me everything."

"Of course," Arthur chuckled.

Then, Tamara bit down on her lower lip as she remembered that after taking her time about disclosing her initial discussions with Arthur Flemming she'd almost severed the LPS council. There were only three of them left now and they needed to stand united. With this in mind she said, "Arthur, I have a few things I need to take care of right now. Would you mind if we continue this discussion later, over dinner, say at the Greenery?"

"The Greenery? Right across from the courthouse? Sounds a little risky."

"Perhaps but, whether from friend or foe, there'll be no more hiding."

"Okay then, I'll meet you there at seven."

As soon as Arthur left Tamara called Tom and Jason and invited them along to dinner so that the three council members could hear Flemming's story together. He might not be ready for an audience and seeing the others might spook him but if it did, so be it. Flemming needed to understand that the council stood united.

# Chapter 31

"This isn't the most conducive setting for a private meeting," Tom stated softly as he scanned the bustling restaurant.

Maybe not but at least there will be plenty of witnesses," Tamara responded wryly.

"Witnesses?"

"Yeah in the event Coulter tries to have us bumped off."

"Thanks," Jason said. "As if I'm not nervous enough already without you having to add a comment like that."

"Oh come on, you two. Loosen up." Tamara maintained a brave front despite experiencing her own anxiety wondering where their meeting with Arthur Flemming might take them next.

"I'll try," Jason submitted. "Hey, you know what?" he added in an attempt to take his mind off the danger their investigations and alliances had led them. "I think this is a first for me. I've never had dinner at the Greenery before. I guess that means I'm not the political type ... well, until now anyway."

As Jason spoke they noticed Arthur Flemming enter the restaurant. He stopped at the reception podium and looked around carefully, obviously checking to see if any politicians were there spot him.

"I wonder how many of patrons in the house tonight have had their palms greased by Sir Arthur at one time or another?" Tom mused.

"Stop it, Tom. You swore you'd keep an open mind," Tamara scolded.

Flemming's gaze eventually found Tamara and he started forward until he noticed the two others. He hesitated, startled that she wasn't alone, but then slowly sauntered to their table. "Well, well," he declared. "Such a pleasant surprise, gentlemen."

After an appropriate exchange of greetings the conversation began cautiously as Flemming attempted to gauge how much Tamara intended or, more likely, how much he wanted to share with Sanders and McAlpin. Flemming feared that it was too soon to let too many people in on his dirty secrets. But it was obvious that Tamara meant for him to tell her associates exactly what he had planned to explain to her earlier in the day. And now, if he were to be truly sincere like he had promised, it was time to reveal his account. So Arthur ordered a cocktail and began to methodically describe how certain developers, including himself in one instance, were able to unobtrusively commence large scale projects after quietly acquiring farmland and having it re-zoned under Nathan Coulter's helpful hand.

Each series of transactions essentially began by using a straw man to purchase the farmland just as the council had uncovered in their investigations. "The straw men were used to keep interested parties such as the LPS off our trail," Arthur disclosed. "If someone like myself or John Gardner had made the purchases directly it would have drawn too much attention. Someone would have certainly said 'Hey wait, that land isn't zoned for residential or commercial development and I'm sure that developer doesn't intend on becoming a farmer. Something fishy must be going on.' So instead, we had the straw man make the purchase and then he'd pretend to farm the property for a while. After that, some scheme or another would be used to justify partial development in preparation for the start of a large scale project."

"Didn't anyone follow up on the zoning status?" Jason inquired.

"By the time anyone would have it'd be too late because Coulter had already altered the titles. Remember that the head of records is the County Clerk's political appointee and therefore Coulter could get things changed with barely a wink."

After much additional discussion, Flemming sighed deeply. He shot a grave look at Tamara, then Tom, then Jason and then back to Tom and finally Tamara again. "There's another issue even bigger than the doctored land swaps that I'm about to tell you about. An issue so big that just by itself it would bring Coulter down if enough information were brought to light."

The three LPS members stared back waiting to listen intently. "Well, go on," Tamara coaxed.

"Okay, here goes. Not long after Coulter was elected for the first time, he began working to change the status of Ogle County from Semi-Rural to Mixed-Use,"

"Yes, I remember, and as we all know he was quite successful," Tom added.

"Right, and I was part of the commission that studied the issue and submitted reports to the federal government that concluded the change was necessary."

"How'd you become part of such a commission?" Jason asked.

"Coulter appointed me. He thought that my experience with development in other suburban counties would be helpful and he was right. There were also various Coulter cronies on the commission who helped push through what he wanted. Ultimately, key facts and documents that were attached as appendices to our report were altered to support his position. There was an underlying study thrown in to demonstrate that overall growth in the metropolitan Chicago area outpaced the available space in the collar counties. We dismissed all the space that could easily be made available by rehabbing vacant or underutilized buildings by claiming that over ninety percent of such structures had already been earmarked for rehab. That was obviously false because how much rehab have you actually seen and you know those counties could benefit a ton from a little restoration. Furthermore, we added what was a basically fictitious report to indicate that Ogle County farming provided virtually no incremental value to northern Illinois' agricultural output."

"Didn't anyone question the facts?"

"A few did but I have to admit that we were good. We knew what we could mess with and what we couldn't. It also helped that Coulter lined the pockets of several key federal bureaucrats who held sway with certain legislators. Most legislators don't have time to read the fine print."

"There's something I don't understand about all of this," Tamara said.

"What's that?"

"How does Coulter benefit from all of this? Does he demand a large kickback anytime you development sorts start a new project?"

"Surprisingly, not really. Occasionally, as one of the large projects gets underway, a developer will throw him a plot that he'll put in a land trust so that no one sees his name on the title. He'll rent out the property or sell it and convert to cash. But, for the most part, the only reason he's done all of this is for purpose of feeding his ego. More development means more people and more business to rule over and it means a larger tax base to manage."

"So the entire county is being paved over for the sake of feeding one man's ego?"

"I don't know if I'd go quite that far. There are several greedy individuals and corporations as well as countless enabling parties who also play a role."

"So what's to become of you if you blow the whistle?" Tom asked thoughtfully.

"I'm not sure but hopefully I don't end up next to Andy Cemanski. I'm sorry, that probably sounded rather uncaring. Actually, I don't think I'll have to worry about Coulter as long as my story doesn't leak before it gets to the press and to the Feds. He wouldn't dare try to hush me or dole out revenge if the matter becomes high profile. It'd be way too obvious that he's responsible. On the other hand, my blowing the whistle won't necessarily provide immunity from federal prosecution. I'll end up implicating myself in certain crimes and could end up serving jail time."

"There's one more thing I don't understand, Arthur," Tom added.

"I knew you couldn't have exhausted your questions yet, professor."

"Why are you giving up on using the Mississippian burial grounds as a way to expose Coulter? That seems to be a less risky proposition for you personally. If the citizenry finds out he's been covering up the existence of a historical Native American site there's bound to be a certain degree of public outrage. That, in turn, could lead to investigations into other questionable dealings that won't necessarily lead to you."

"I don't think there's going to be much to uncover at Meador Farms."

"Why's that?"

"Well," Flemming started rather sheepishly, "There really aren't any Indian burial grounds."

"What?" Jason questioned indignantly.

"Uh, that was an issue that I wasn't exactly upfront with you either. My intentions were good, however. I thought we could use it as a stall tactic to divert Coulter and Gardner while we gained momentum in other areas. I apologize but I also had to use the burial grounds as a guise to interest you folks in working with me. I thought that by now you might have figured it was a hoax, professor."

Sanders stared at Flemming forlornly, not really seeing him. Flemming didn't comprehend his disappointment nor did Tamara or Jason for the moment. Tom could never quite come to believe that the burial grounds actually existed but he clung to the possibility in hopes that the Meador Farms property could be saved. Before Tom could respond Tamara erupted. "Geez, Arthur! What were you going to do let the LPS play the fool by making an issue over a fake burial site while you snatched up our land?"

"Please, not so loud," Flemming requested as he glanced around the restaurant. "No, Tamara, in answer to your question. That wasn't my intention at all. I was going to tell you about the hoax eventually. I still think it might have worked. Like the professor said, it was a safer plan from my standpoint. But not after what Coulter's done to you. It would be too dangerous to toy with him now. We don't have time. The only way to stop him is for me to tell the world everything I know about his illegal acts."

Tom had to agree with Flemming's reasoning but he was still curious about the burial grounds hoax. "How did you make Coulter think that the Native American site was a real issue?" he asked, only marginally satisfied that he wasn't the only one to buy into the ruse.

"It was easier than I thought it would be. As you know, there are burial grounds down by Cahokia. I gathered some literature on the site and took it to a county employee who I knew would take the information to Coulter immediately even though he swore he wouldn't of course. I was careful to make sure that all references to present day, common name locations were excluded from the documents and I didn't dare leave copies behind. He only got to read it once, which was critical because the location reference was a legal description: range and section and so forth. The type of description that only a surveyor would understand. As a result, the only thing this guy concentrated on was the fact that a burial ground actually existed. He didn't realize that the property I described, Meador Farms, didn't match the one in the legal description."

"No one else checked the facts?"

"Again, just like the other doctored reports I told you about, the answer is amazingly no. I think that it helped that I shared the information with another one of Coulter's toads a few days later. So then like that, a low key, unsubstantiated rumor essentially became common knowledge in the Clerk's office."

"Wow."

"Yeah, wow."

The group continued talking for several more minutes before they agreed that it was best to adjourn before drawing further attention. As Tamara drove home she couldn't help but to wonder if Arthur was truly sincere. She hoped he was, the future of the LPS almost relied on the fact that he was, but she prepared herself for the contrary. Then, as Tamara made the last turn into her neighborhood she became conscious that she had been followed.

# Chapter 32

The lights reflected ominously in her rearview mirror. She made a left onto a court rather than a right to her town home and then turned into the first driveway as her pursuer passed by on the main street. The vehicle seemed to slow as the driver undoubtedly spotted where she had stopped but its taillights disappeared around a curve in the road and Tamara quickly reversed out of the driveway and headed back toward home. The maneuver was likely in vain because the stalker already knew her address, she was almost certain, but the effort was worth a try.

She contacted Tom who was still on his way home. "I've been followed. How 'bout you?"

"Not that I can tell. Are you still in your vehicle?" he asked worriedly.

"Yes."

"Keep driving. Head toward my house but only take major arteries. Ride with traffic."

"I think I may have lost him. I'm going to try to get in my garage before he spots me again."

"I'm on my way over then."

"Better not, you could end up leading them right to both of us. I'll call that detective who came over to investigate the note instead. He said to call if I ever felt threatened." Tamara's heart was pounding but her thought process remained clear.

"Can you trust him?"

"I know what you're thinking, but if we can't trust him our fates are inevitable anyway."

Tom took a deep breath. "Okay, unfortunately you're probably right. But I'll hang on the connection until you make contact with him. In the meantime, I'm going to drive in your direction so I can get to your place a little faster if needed. Don't worry I won't get too close."

Tamara waited uneasily for the detective to arrive constantly peeking out the windows on all sides of her town house. So far there was no sign that the predator had picked up her trail again. Then, she caught a glimpse of a vehicle with no lights on inching up the street in front of her home. She was certain that the automobile wasn't the same as the one she had shaken earlier. Eventually it passed her drive and then stopped in front of her neighbor's house. A small man emerged from the vehicle and angled across the lawn directly toward Tamara's door. The man was unimpressive, disheveled in appearance, yet under the circumstances his figure cast a menacing shadow. As he drew closer Tamara recognized him.

Despite the tension, Tamara found the situation somewhat amusing. "What's with the cloak and dagger entrance, detective?" she said as she opened the door.

"Sorry, Ma'am. In my business, however, there's no reason to announce my arrival. There's always a chance I might be able to sneak up on a few suspects,"

Tamara showed Detective Robbins through the door and offered him a cup of coffee. They sat down at the kitchen table and he asked a few standard questions including whether she recognized the make and model of the vehicle that was pursuing her. He also inquired whether she'd contacted anyone else since sensing that she was being followed. She told the detective that she'd been in touch with Tom Sanders. The detective was familiar with the professor because they'd been introduced due to the potential link between the note to Tamara and the break-in at the Sanders house.

Then Robbins was silent for several moments as he gazed absently around the room and into the darkness outside the kitchen window. Finally, he asked, "Where's your vehicle, Ma'am?"

"In the garage," Tamara answered nonchalantly.

"Do you mind if I have a look at it?"

"Not at all."

Several minutes later Robbins emerged from the garage and said, "Ms. Hopkins, can you please come out there with me for a moment?"

Tamara agreed to his request and followed the detective back to the garage where she watched as he extracted a tiny device from beneath the front wheelbase of her vehicle.

"It's a tracking system," he said answering Tamara's question before she could ask. "The manufacture of these systems was made illegal long ago after years of abuse and an outcry against their invasion on privacy. Nevertheless, if someone really wants to get their hands on one of these babies they can be found."

"My God! So they know where I am at all times?"

"Pretty much."

"What now? Can you use that thing to track back to the people who put it there?"

"Not really, so if I were you I'm not sure that I'd stay here tonight. But I do have another idea. I'll plant the device in your garage and then you can drive off and check into a hotel somewhere for a few days. The tracking system will be indicating to them that you haven't moved. They'll think you're holing up, afraid to leave the house."

"Then what?"

"They might get frustrated and come poking around. We'll keep a constant surveillance and see who shows up."

"Who is 'we', detective?"

"My department," he answered misunderstanding where she was going with her question and wondering if Hopkins was less together than he'd given her credit for.

"How do we know one of them isn't part of this?"

"What do you mean?"

"How do you know one of the boys or girls in your department doesn't work for Coulter?"

"Well, technically, I guess we all work for Coulter," Robbins responded with a puzzled look.

"Do you understand what I'm trying to tell you, Detective Robbins?" Tamara asked with an intense stare.

"I think I'm beginning to."

"Yes, in all likelihood, it's Nathan Coulter who is the head man behind this intimidation ring. He seems to have a problem with anyone who might have an interest in land preservation in this county."

Robbins turned his face into an odd contortion of lines and wrinkles and scratched the back of his neck. Then he replied, "I'll place only my most trustworthy comrades on this assignment."

"Good, but can I trust you?" Tamara asked looking Robbins directly in the eye. Even though she found herself to come to like the man she had to ask him that question. The rather small detective was quirky but she sensed, or at least she hoped, that he was honorable and devoted to his profession more so than to the politics of county government.

"Well, Ms. Hopkins, if you can't trust me, your problems are even bigger than you think."

"Funny but I think that I've already told myself the same thing. Okay then, let's start working your plan."

"Okay," Robbins responded quietly. "You realize though, if we do catch one of Coulter's men in this operation things could get rather sticky."

Before she left her town house, Tamara told the detective she wanted to call Sanders back. When she got Tom on the line she informed him about the plan and recommended that he go home and get a good night's rest before they reconvened. Overhearing her side of the conversation, Robbins said, "Make sure that the professor doesn't visit you at your hotel."

"What? Why not?"

"Chances are pretty good that they've mounted a tracking device on his vehicle as well."

# Chapter 33

Up until that morning, Tom was coping fairly well with the idea that his vehicle was "bugged." Over the last several days he'd only traveled back and forth between home and the university anyway. Since Coulter's thugs already knew how to find those locations, if there was a tracking device attached to his vehicle it wasn't providing them with much information. Besides, Tom wasn't about to tamper with anything until Detective Robbins' experiment with the device left behind in Tamara's garage had been concluded. He didn't want to raise Coulter's suspicions.

By now though, Tom was itching to get out to see Meador Farms again. He'd fallen in love with the contour of the land there and the sensation he received from its vastness that was as if he were stepping into another region or a different era. But he couldn't run the risk of being tracked to the property as long as the smallest chance remained that Coulter hadn't dismissed the burial ground rumor. The hoax was the only way development might be delayed.

After Andy's death, Sanders used his research to overcome his despondency and the Native American burial grounds were what remained to stir his emotions in order that he might lead the LPS in a fight to save the land. How disappointed he'd been when Flemming told them that there weren't any burial grounds on the property. His research had effectively ascertained that conclusion already but until Arthur's announcement the professor hadn't been ready to close the door on possibility. Now, Tom lamented, the hope that lingered for Meador Farms was hanging by a thread. If the hoax had run its course what ammunition did he have left?

When Tamara arrived at Tom's office that morning she found him irritable. "What's your problem?" she asked playfully. "I'm the one who hasn't slept in my own bed for the last three nights."

"I'm sorry, Tam. I guess I'm just frustrated. It's like we're trapped searching for direction again," Tom replied, eyes slowly casting downward, losing contact.

"Believe me, I know how you feel."

Tamara's mood, blunt but good-humored, is what he needed. She seemed to be coping with adversity so why shouldn't he? "Okay, no more wallowing," Tom announced as he sat up straighter. "So, do you think Arthur Flemming has gone to the Feds yet?"

"I don't know. But I was thinking, maybe we should take what Arthur told us to the Rural Reformers. That way, if Arthur never gets to the Feds, Double R can still use Coulter's frauds and bribes as a campaign issue."

Tom raised an eyebrow. "You'd compromise Arthur like that?"

"Well, um, yes. I don't mean to sound ruthless but why not? He's used us before so how do we trust him now and believe that he's actually going to carry through with blowing the whistle on Coulter?"

"That's another matter. How do we trust him? If we give his story to the Rural Reformers and it can't be substantiated it could backfire on them."

Tamara considered his point and then it came to her. "Just like the Indian burial grounds could have backfired on us. Is that what's really bothering you, Tom?"

"I suppose. I really thought we had a chance to save that property."

"We still can."

"It's only a matter of time before Coulter and Gardner find out that there aren't any burial grounds. But I'm starting to sound like Robert. I've become caught up with worrying about Meador Farms rather than focusing on the bigger picture. I need to move on and not get upset if we lose this one parcel."

Tamara looked at him understandingly. "We don't know what will become of the Rural Reformers, Nathan Coulter or Arthur Flemming, for that matter, so our mission may yet come down to saving one property at a time. You said it yourself," she implored, "those lands are worth fighting for, burial grounds or no burial grounds. Come on, Tom, I've heard you speak. Capture that feeling again and lead us forward, forty acres at a time."

"Okay, coach, I'll do it. But I sure hope that they don't start shooting again."

Before Tamara could respond she received a call on her direct link. It was Detective Robbins.

"We nabbed a fellow lurking about your place last night. I didn't want to call you until we had an opportunity to run him through the paces to see what we could learn. I'm not sure I should tell you this… but it looks like it could be one of the main man's boys."

"One of Coulter's boys? How do you know? Did you get him to squeal?" Tamara asked excitedly drawing Tom's attention to her conversation.

"Are you kidding?" Robbins responded dryly from the other end. "That'll never happen but I've been in this business long enough to know who's who. Don't get too excited though because you can bet we'll never officially connect the dots all the way to the top."

"Maybe you can give us the leads and we can 'unofficially' go to the top," Tamara suggested.

"Ms. Hopkins, do you realize how dangerous this game is?"

Tamara looked over at Tom and then considered Andy's fate. "Yes, I think I do," she answered. "Is it at least safe for me to go home?"

"They'll lay low for a while," the detective said. "So yeah, for the time being, you're safe there. I may be out of a job after this bust, but you'll be safe there."

# Chapter 34

**B**efore he even knew what he was going to say, Tom had made an appointment and was on his way to GDC's offices. His mission was clear, however: convince John Gardner to turn Meador Farms over to the LPS. While he drove Tom formulated a rough scheme of what it would take to accomplish his aim. GDC's principal coveted the eighty acres the LPS had acquired on Prairie Parkway and, though he hated the idea of giving the property away, Tom needed a lure. Offering Prairie Parkway in return might be the only way of enticing Gardner to bite at the notion of relinquishing Meadow Farms. One thing was certain; Gardner wasn't about to miraculously donate the land to the LPS as a result of a sudden affinity for the preservation cause.

Saving Meador Farms had become a more significant priority because Tom realized that the LPS had a better chance of curbing overall development in the west. The tide had already washed over the central county where Prairie Parkway was situated and they wouldn't be able to accumulate sizable holdings there. The LPS was already land-locked between Gardner on one side and Flemming's property on the other. Counting on Arthur Flemming to merge his one hundred and sixty acres with their Prairie Parkway holding would be foolhardy at this point. In the near term, per chance Arthur did blow the whistle on Nathan Coulter he'd likely be adverse to the further risk of being caught cooperating with the LPS. Quite possibly, Flemming would disappear altogether and they'd never hear from him again.

"So Mr. Sanders," Gardner crooned as Tom was escorted into his office, "you've finally come to see me. Please, have a seat."

Tom subtly furrowed his brow. "I didn't realize that you'd been expecting my call for so long, Mr. Gardner."

"Not expecting necessarily but perhaps hoping. I'm sure you heard that we met with your associate, Sonnvoldt. He didn't give us much feedback so I eventually sent a message directly to Ms. Hopkins' office to let her know that I was interested in purchasing her—or perhaps it's your—Prairie Parkway property. I didn't get any reply at all to that communiqué. I was a little insulted at first but then I realized that it's just business. One doesn't have time to take every call that one receives."

An artful jab, Sanders thought. The man seems to have done his homework regarding the company I keep besides. "Well, thank you for taking my call," Tom responded.

"No problem. I do the best I can to be accessible, Mr. Sanders—or should I be saying Dr. Sanders?"

"Whichever makes you feel more comfortable is fine with me."

"That's very accommodating," Gardner responded condescendingly. "Anyway, what can I do for you today, professor?"

"I'd like to purchase Meador Farms," Tom answered without hesitation.

Gardner raised his eyebrows. "That's interesting. Hmm, I was hoping you were here to sell property. I hadn't imagined you were in the market to buy more property."

"I may be willing to sell property as long as I can acquire Meador Farms," Tom said calmly.

"Meador Farms is an expensive piece of real estate, professor. Maybe the academic life is more lucrative than I've been told. Oh, but that's right, your wife probably makes a good buck being a high-powered attorney and all."

Sanders shifted in his chair almost involuntarily, hopefully not obvious enough for Gardner to notice. He was uneasy over Gardner's seeming familiarity with his LPS associates, his career and now his wife. Then he responded quickly attempting to pass through his moment of discomfort. "So, what's your asking price?"

"You don't beat around the bush."

"I try not to, Mr. Gardner."

"Okay, but first tell me about the property that you'd like to sell."

"I didn't necessarily say I wanted to sell it; however, I would consider swapping the Prairie Parkway property for Meador Farms."

"You would…but I thought your colleague owned that land on Prairie Parkway. How can you swap her property? You're not representing the LPS, are you, professor? Because I don't think your organization is legally recognized in this county," Gardner pointed out in a clever shift of tone in attempt to gain negotiating leverage.

Ah, I'm dealing with a true Machiavellian, Tom marveled as he looked over the crafty developer before responding. "Let's just say that Ms. Hopkins and I are partners with regard to certain real estate investments."

"I see, but why the sudden interest in Meador Farms?"

"I'm a history professor, Mr. Gardner, and that property holds certain historical relevance. The remains buried there might teach me something more about early American culture, if you know what I mean."

Now Sanders was the one playing coy knowing Gardner would assume that he was referring to the Indian claim. Tom hoped that Gardner would interpret his statement to mean that he was intending to use the burial grounds as a negotiating chip and that he wouldn't be afraid to expose the issue if he didn't receive cooperation. Whether or not Gardner would take the bait was questionable and was predicated on the chance that he hadn't already discovered that the burial grounds were a hoax. Sanders sat pensively waiting for Gardner's reaction.

"I hope you aren't suggesting a straight up swap of the properties," Gardner said without giving any indication what he knew about the alleged Mississippian site. "You and Ms. Hopkins must understand that Meador Farms is several times the size of your property."

"True; however, the price of real estate per acre is quite a bit higher in the central county compared to where the Meador property is located. Furthermore, you don't have the historical issue to contend with on Prairie Parkway."

"Hmm, yes. But, you know what, I was beginning to grow fond of Meador Farms." Now it seemed Gardner was calling his bluff or possibly, Tom considered, he was playing his own bluff.

The professor remained cool recognizing the importance of staying mum. A comeback now would only serve to work against the offer he'd already laid out. Then Gardner spoke again. "No, professor. You'll have to offer something more for me to consider parting with Meador Farms."

Tom wasn't altogether unprepared for such a response. He understood that Gardner had built his empire largely on his abilities as a shrewd dealmaker. Gardner had also pointed out the obvious: Meador Farms was a substantially larger parcel than what the LPS owned on Prairie Parkway.

In contemplation of Gardner's response, Sanders had searched his soul and considered whether what Tamara told him was more than just flattery? Did he really have the ability to lead the LPS in a fight to save Meador Farms? If he did his success likely hinged upon inspiring donors and raising funds to buy the property outright at whatever outlandish price Gardner was about to demand. But, first, he wanted to try one more angle. His mother had willed him a decaying apartment building in Kane County. Although the structure was in disrepair it was in area that showed signs of gentrification. The property had some value and perhaps Gardner would consider accepting it along with the Prairie Parkway land in exchange for Meador Farms.

Sanders sighed, "All right, even though I hate to do this, I'm prepared to increase my offer."

"I'm listening," Gardner replied.

"I own a twelve-unit apartment building in the heart of Kane County. You can take that plus Prairie Parkway."

"An apartment building? How old is it?"

"Forty-five to fifty years old by my recollection."

"What kind of shape is it in? Is it fully rented?"

"I believe it's fifty percent occupied right now. But that might be the upside for you. GDC can rehab the building and then sell it for a tidy profit or garner a nice income stream by continuing to rent the units."

"We don't do rehab, professor," Gardner said curtly.

"You should consider it. Rehab can be profitable plus it conserves open space."

"I don't bother with that kind of nonsense. That's the beauty of prosperity, professor. Conservation is not my concern. I take an open landscape and build from scratch without having to worry about what the last guy left behind."

Gardner's comments left Sanders feeling hollow. Obviously, the developer had no regard for the environment, particularly if it stood in the way of profits. The professor tilted his head and asked, "Tell me, Mr. Gardner, do you gather any enjoyment from nature? Do you take pleasure from noticing which trees bud first in the springtime, from smelling fresh air after a cleansing rainstorm or from watching a deer lope across the meadow?"

"I don't know. I don't spend much time thinking about those sorts of things."

"Really? What about your children and your children's children? What if there's no more land left for them to even consider building on?"

"Interesting question. You're starting to make me feel like I'm attending one of your classes. Give me time to think… Okay, my answer is that I believe the human race is very resourceful. They'll figure out what to do when the time comes. Getting back to your offer though—I'm not interested in your apartment building. Do you have any other land, particularly something located in Ogle County?"

Sanders turned sullen. He and Gardner were on totally different wavelengths and, no, he didn't have anything else to offer. The only other property he owned was his homestead, which contained the orchard, terraced cropland and his secret forest and hidden prairie. He wasn't about to give that up. "There's nothing else."

"What about the other Prairie Parkway parcel, the one that Pinnacle Development purchased? It seems as if Arthur Flemming has become your buddy. Perhaps he can contribute his land to the offer."

What does he know about our involvement with Arthur Flemming? What doesn't he know, Tom wondered feeling hopeless? "I'm not affiliated with Pinnacle Development," he choked out. "I hardly think that it would be appropriate for me to offer one of their properties in a trade."

"That's too bad. Well then, do you have any cash? Your eighty acres alone just aren't enough for me to consider selling Meador Farms."

The professor exhaled. I can't give up now, he thought. Now is the time to test my mettle. He had to raise the troops and do what was necessary to save Meador Farms.

"Yes, we have plenty of cash," Sanders stated confidently using his own loose interpretation of *plenty* knowing that it probably fell far short of Gardner's expectations. "Of course, we'll only pay what we feel is reasonable," he added.

"What's reasonable?"

"I've already made what I thought was a reasonable offer," Sanders stated cautiously, attempting to learn the art of negotiation on the fly, as he stared down the man considered master of all Ogle County real estate dealers.

With surprisingly little hesitation Gardner blurted, "Two point five million."

"Fine," Tom shot back. "I'll take that amount under consideration and see if I can make it work. I'll get back to you within a week."

The disparate trading partners exchanged pleasantries as they stood and shook hands and then Tom Sanders made his way out of GDC through the stately double doors contemplating what had transpired. He was surprised by Gardner's counteroffer. Considering Gardner's posturing he'd expected to be asked to pay more than an additional two point five million. Maybe I'm better at this game than I thought I'd be, Tom considered as he fought off the smile quivering to come upon his face. But, on the other hand, he had no idea where he'd come up with even that kind of money. "I will though," he exclaimed quietly as he slid behind the wheel of his vehicle.

John Gardner watched through his office window until Sanders drove out of sight and then immediately called for Cristin Anelli and Julie Dubose. When they entered his office he barked, "What's happening with our development permit?"

"Coulter's man says they won't be ready to issue anything until this matter regarding the Indian burial ground is closed," Julie Dubose answered.

Gardner quickly shifted his glare toward his information director. "Cristin, you told me that you've found absolutely no evidence that a damn graveyard exists."

"That is correct, sir."

"You know I hate it when you call me sir," Gardner sneered, briefly losing his focus.

"I know, sir." Anelli responded in monotone.

Gardner ignored Anelli's dry attempt at amusing herself at his expense and returned his concentration to Meador Farms and the burial grounds. "Haven't Coulter's people figured out that it's a hoax?"

"I would have thought so but…"

"Fine. I'm going down to Coulter's office to tell him we're breaking ground next week, with or without a permit."

"Do you think that's such a good idea, John?" Julie Dubose counseled. "Being that the election is right around the corner, he might not be too receptive to being pushed around."

"Yeah, you're probably right," Gardner conceded. "Don't worry; I won't push him too far. I'll just talk nice-like and mention that he owes us one. But he's must have figured out that we've been chasing ghosts. Somebody's planted that burial ground rumor."

# Chapter 35

"Arthur actually came through," she mumbled to herself as she read the headline floating across her screen. "Coulter Found Tilting County Landscape." Tamara continued scanning through the article intently. "Nathan Coulter, Ogle County Clerk, has been accused of manipulating congressional reports and bribing government officials in order to pass through a reclassification of the county's federal status from Semi-Rural to Mixed Business and Residential," the news piece reported. "Further charges allege that the County Clerk illegally concealed zoning changes to allow large residential and commercial projects to be built over land previously designated for agricultural purposes. Coulter is suspected of receiving kickbacks and political favors from the beneficiary developers. These allegations are untimely for the sitting County Clerk currently seeking re-election for an unprecedented fourth term."

Further west, from her home near the Rock River, Marina Sanders came across the same article. Tom hinted about the possibility of disparaging information coming forward concerning Nathan Coulter; however, when she asked him to tell her more just this morning, he seemed less confident that public disclosure would ever surface. But now, here it was for thousands upon thousands of citizens to see. This is amazing, she thought as she read more.

"The allegations are not likely to be substantiated prior to April's election," the reporter noted. "Nonetheless, they could potentially swing certain voters as they cast their ballots in a proceeding until now considered perfunctory."

"Maybe this will help the public recognize the man for the low life, deceptive tyrant that he truly is," Marina declared when she called her husband at the University to find out whether he'd seen the news piece.

"This couldn't have come at a better time, honey," Tom chortled as Marina read to him from the article. "Tomorrow evening I go before the membership to ask for approval to use our reserve funds to help acquire that beautiful property I've been telling you about. I'll have to beg for a few donations to complete the deal but this news might convince more members to open their pocket books. By the way, does your firm have any wealthy clients who'd like to throw in a few dollars to help us acquire the property; perhaps they could consider it an investment in the future?"

"I can ask around; however, I think we'll find that most of those clients prefer their returns to be in cold, hard cash rather than in the form of the warm, fuzzy feeling you get from land preservation."

"All right, never mind. I keep forgetting that point," Tom said jokingly but in full realization that raising money for the Meador Farms purchase would be difficult even after the revelations about Coulter.

At Gardner Development Company the news was also received with great interest. Cristin Anelli was the first one to bring the story to John Gardner's attention.

Her boss wasn't necessarily shocked by the nature of the charges but Anelli could sense he was concerned. For several moments Gardner sat pensively his mind spiraling through the various dealings he'd had with Nathan Coulter over the course of his career. "So who's the source behind these allegations?" he finally asked.

"The article referenced unnamed sources but I've put together a few connections. It had to have been Arthur Flemming."

Gardner was surprised by this part of the news. "No kidding? Okay, call everybody together. We need to talk about this."

When his management team was assembled Gardner said haughtily, " So Arthur Flemming has turned state's evidence on the Honorable Nathan Coulter. Hmm, shows you what lust can do to a man."

"Sir?"

"I mean come on, why else would he have squealed? He must have it bad for the Hopkins woman. She put him up to it. Nothing else makes sense because its not like Flemming didn't benefit from the crimes he's accusing Coulter of committing."

"Yeah, it does seem strange that a guy like Flemming would come forward on something like this," Gardner's Chief Financial Officer agreed, "particularly coming so close to the election."

Then John Gardner's face turned dour. "Well, the real reason I called you all in here is to discuss what effect this revelation has on us."

His managers glanced at one another guardedly before the Operations Director spoke up. "I don't see how this should have any impact on us, unless, of course, Coulter's voted out of office. But that's not going to happen," he added emphatically.

"My question is, do you think there's any chance our name will surface related to any of the illegal land deals alluded to in the article?"

After Gardner made his clarification he looked over his staff carefully, beginning to regret that he'd asked. Julie Dubose was the only one present who he had confided in regarding the details of the Daniel's Crossing transaction. He suspected that Cristin Anelli had probably made a connection on what had transpired when ferreting through some other transaction or another. She seemed to know about everything else, but if Anelli had ever pieced together the dubious chain of events leading up to the Daniel's Crossing Development she'd never brought them up. Thankfully, Gardner thought, because he believed that it was best that very few people ever understood the details behind the deal.

"Which one's should we be worrying about, John?" the CFO asked.

Gardner used the question as an opportunity to recover from having divulged more than he'd liked. "That's what I'm asking you. None of you got us involved in something you shouldn't have?"

There was no response.

"Good! Let's keep pressing forward with our current business. I want to get Meador Farms started as soon as possible. Coulter's office is going to be too busy worrying about damage control to have time to fool around with development permits and we just can't wait for them any longer."

# Chapter 36

If ever an assembly was needed now was the time, Tom convinced himself. Initially, he worried that the members might think he was arranging the meeting as a campaign stunt. But then so be it, he thought, because what needed to be said and what needed to be decided had to be done so quickly and, if he was being self serving, it was in order to save the land that he had come to love rather than to save his post as President of the LPS.

The president didn't call many special sessions and ample warning was provided whenever he had. But that wasn't the case this time. However, considering the short notice a remarkable number of members had confirmed their attendance. There would be one hundred and thirty-two gathered in all.

The last member contacted for Tom's urgent meeting received barely three hours notice. "Where's it going to be held?" questioned the perplexed member.

"The Westwind Hotel in DeKalb County," the delegate answered.

"Why over there?"

"DeKalb County doesn't have a prohibition on our assemblies."

Tom picked up Tamara Hopkins on his way to the meeting so he could brief her on his Meador Farms purchase proposal while they rode. He was nervous afraid the members wouldn't understand the importance.

"Don't worry." Tamara assured him. "Just explain it to them like you did to me and Jason."

"I don't know if I can."

As they crossed the county line Tamara changed the subject hoping to take Tom's mind off of his presentation. "What if we gave the society a new name?" she suggested, only partially in jest. " Maybe we wouldn't be banned from operating in Ogle County any longer."

"I think Andy would roll over in his grave if we gave in and changed our name," Tom replied without much consideration.

"Sure he would, but if I'm not mistaken he was the main 'subversive' who got our group outlawed in the first place," Tamara said taking a playful jab at the old warrior as if he were still there to listen.

"That's right and I think he was damn proud of it."

Tamara's plan seemed to work. Tom had stopped dwelling on his speech and was more relaxed by the time they arrived at the hotel's conference center. After a general welcoming, Tom gaveled the meeting to order at 7:30 p.m. The first item of business was to establish election procedures for a new term for the LPS council. Sanders recommended that the society delay their internal proceedings until June to give time for the dust to settle on the more overriding county election, which was now only two weeks away. The membership seemed to nod uniformly in agreement and then Tom informed them that, "after much soul searching, I have decided to seek re-election as the society's president. Tamara Hopkins and Jason McAlpin have also agreed to run for new terms as council members."

When Tom asked if there were any other members wishing to run for president, one man raised his hand. When he made the same inquiry regarding the other council positions, three individuals raised their hands and their names were duly recorded. This meant that there would be only five candidates running for the four non-presidential seats. So no matter what, one of the incumbents was guaranteed re-election. However, if Tom were ousted as president, Jason or Tamara might be serving alone on an otherwise new council.

Robert Sonnvoldt was at the meeting and when asked he stood and firmly stated that, "my resignation as councilman was and still is intended to be permanent. However," he added, "I still consider myself to be a proud member of the Land Preservation Society."

Robert's presence and his statement elicited several more questions from the gallery. Some members believed that it was important to understand the reason behind Robert's resignation. They wanted to know if his quitting was a reflection of his feelings toward the other council members. "This could be relevant to our decision making process. Were there any conflicts of interest that we should know about?" one of the members inquired. Sonnvoldt assured the crowd that his resignation had been solely for personal reasons, which as such he felt there was no need to elaborate further. Tamara breathed an inaudible sigh of relief when the questioning was complete and Robert had taken his seat.

The next item of business focused on the previous day's news story attacking Nathan Coulter's ethical character. The entire membership believed he was corrupt but until yesterday they had been resigned to their collective fate that he'd never be indicted. Finally somebody with inside information had the guts to speak up. Prior to the meeting, the room was abuzz about the opportunities that the king's fall might present for the LPS and now, when Sanders brought the subject back to the forefront, the energy level elevated even higher. Tom called for "order" twice as the discussion progressed and eventually concluded the matter by declaring, "we can't be certain of the impact these disclosures will have on the county elections. Coulter was so far ahead when the last opinion poll was released that it would still take a miracle for the Rural Reformers to pull out the race. But it's our duty to help nudge that miracle along because we know one thing for sure: that man will continue to be our biggest enemy until he's voted from office. So get to your polling place and cast a ballot and make sure your, family, friends and associates are well aware of this news piece and get them out to vote too, even if it means carrying them to the polls on your back."

"Hooray for that!" came a shout from the gallery.

Then came time to present the matter Sanders was most anxious to address: the acquisition of Meador Farms. First, Tom provided the members with a description of the property from the stream that meandered through the meadow to the mix of pasture and forestland to the ridgeline running across the southern and western boundaries that provided a stunning view of the surrounding countryside. Then he graphically depicted the general environs where Meador Farms was situated starting with the gentle rise in elevation west of the Rock River that marked the gateway to the area. He noted the quaint village on the horizon rising like a postcard out of the rural scenery. "This tiny region," he proclaimed, " is like no other found in Ogle County."

After describing the property, Tom outlined the financial requirements to complete the acquisition. "We'll have to trade the Prairie Parkway property and, in addition, I'm requesting the release of two million dollars from our general reserve fund. Furthermore, I'd like each of us to generously reach into our pockets so that we can raise an additional five hundred thousand to support the balance of the asking price."

"Preposterous!" screamed the man who would be opposing Sanders in the LPS election. "You're proposing that we release a property we fought hard to obtain plus drain our general reserve for a few hundred acres of land. Have you lost sight of the big picture, President Sanders?"

Tom stared steadfastly at the man, took a deep breath and responded, "No, sir, I don't believe that I have."

Sanders description of Meador Farms and his explanation of the need to purchase the property were convincing to most, but after being brought to task by his presidential challenger he seemed to reach within for something more. From that moment, Tamara and Jason sat in awe as they witnessed for a second time that certain gleam and those mesmerizing oratory skills normally hidden well below the surface of the professor's countenance. Sanders proceeded to explain to the man, as well as all who were gathered, that the purchase of Meador Farms was essential to preserving any remaining hope of saving Ogle County from being swallowed into the abyss of suburbia as had not only DeKalb, Kane, Kendall and Grundy Counties, but also as had countless other counties throughout the United States. "If we don't hold the line here, where will we hold the line?" Sanders challenged his constituents.

His lone dissenter remained skeptical. "What is it about that land, Professor Sanders? I still don't understand how it's any more important than any other property on that side of the river."

"I'm not sure that it is. Perhaps it represents just one small brick. But perhaps we allow them to loosen that brick and the entire wall crumbles."

Tamara stood and shouted, "You're right! Once Gardner starts adding more and more homes on Meador Farms the whole area will go. Other developers will jump in to exploit the commercial desires of the new residents. You all know the scenario. New homeowners move farther out to get more property for a cheaper price and to enjoy a bit of the country life, but before long they loathe the fact that they have to travel more than five minutes to shop. Then, they insist there needs to be a trendy restaurant around the corner and finally someone convinces them they can lower their tax payments by luring a little business and industry to the area. Of course, that someone always forgets to mention all of the other infrastructure that the residents will end up paying for after that."

When she finished speaking Tom let her comments sink in for a few seconds before addressing the gallery again. "Thank you, Tamara. You make an excellent point. Now, I'd like to open the floor for further questions before we take a vote to approve the proposed acquisition of the Meador Farms property. Since we have a quorum of the membership present, a two-thirds majority will suffice for passing the measures necessary. If you haven't already guessed, I'm fully in favor of the purchase of this property. I hope you feel the same way."

There was hush amongst the crowd when Sanders was done speaking and then came a rising murmur until a voice shouted, "We're with you, Tom!"

But before another word the doors on both sides of the room flung open violently. County police rushed in forming picket lines along opposite walls before the commanding officer swaggered through the entrance to the right of the podium. "This assembly shall come to a close!" he ordered.

"What's going on?" a member wailed.

"There's no permit for this assembly. Please disperse immediately!"

Obviously Nathan Coulter, learning of the LPS meeting, had reached his cozy DeKalb County counterpart who, in turn, called in his forces to order a cease and desist. After a clamoring amongst the members they slowly filed out of the conference center. Tom Sanders was detained at the front of the room where Tamara Hopkins and Jason McAlpin refused to leave his side.

"You were the presiding officer at this meeting?" the police chief asked Sanders.

"Yes," Tom responded coolly.

"I understand that you're a professor over at DeKalb University," the chief said smugly pretending to know all that went on in his jurisdiction.

"Yes."

"This could be very embarrassing to you in front of the administration."

"How so?"

"You, presiding over an illegal gathering."

"Me, exercising my right to freedom of speech and assembly. Sir, I'd think you should be the one to be embarrassed."

"Okay, professor," the officer concluded realizing Sanders refused to be moved by his bluster. "We just need to take down some information and then we'll have you and your associates on your way home."

Sanders failed to see the relevance of most of the questions but he was patient and answered what he felt was appropriate. When the chief had finished with them and they were on their way, Tom and Tamara rode in silence. Finally, Tamara exploded. "I can't believe the nerve of that officer. How could he even suggest that they had a legal right to break up our meeting? Their only authority came in the form of the weapons they carried. If we were really the subversive group that Coulter contends there would have been a bloody battle in that room!"

"Yes, I suppose."

"How can you be so calm about this, especially after some of the questions that slimeball asked you? Who the hell does he think he is?"

"There's no point in getting upset with him, Tamara. The poor chap was informed of certain facts, if we can call them that, but he probably had no idea why his boss rang him up from down at the county building and ordered him to break up our meeting. Perhaps even sadder, his boss probably didn't understand the purpose of their mission, either. In all likelihood, he was honoring a political chip that Coulter was cashing in."

"That is sad...and scary, too," Tamara responded somberly. "Does Nathan Coulter really have that much control over our lives? How much longer must we endure his repression and harassment?"

# Chapter 37

Public scrutiny surrounding the alleged manipulation of governmental reports and illegal land deals was intensifying. Election day was less than a week away and Nathan Coulter was surlier by the hour. The County Clerk wasn't accustomed to having his authority challenged. However, despite the criticism and doubts, he still led Samuel Anthony by a wide margin in the opinion polls.

"Anthony's office called again to remind us that ample time remains. They still want to arrange a debate," Clayton Addison relayed in a manner suggesting their proposal was worth consideration.

"Why are we wasting time taking calls from those people?" Coulter growled at his aide.

"Perhaps a debate isn't such a bad idea, sir. The people would be provided the opportunity to witness your leadership and wisdom in a head to head comparison with the inexperience of that political neophyte. That'd be sure to put any doubts in their minds to rest."

"That's ridiculous," Coulter scolded. "You won't see me wallowing in the mud with that buffoon."

"I'm sorry, sir. I was just thinking that we really haven't campaigned very much this time around."

"Of course not because I'm the leader. The public knows that and wants that to continue."

"Okay."

"Besides," Coulter added with disgust, "debates are an archaic form of campaigning and a progressive leader should never stoop to such a mockery. Do you know anything about history? Something like a hundred years ago, one of the first political debates to be shown on the viewing screen almost ended the career of a future president. The cameras zoomed in, close up on this Nixon fellow and showed him perspiring and looking like he was about to crap his pants. He lost that election and didn't become president until after a few more campaigns when people finally forgot about the episode."

"We can control those kinds of things now."

"I know we can but I don't trust some of those freaks in the press. They'll pick out one word or one meaningless gesture and make a huge deal out of it. I won't put up with that kind of bullshit."

"I understand. I should have never brought their request to your attention."

Coulter sat quietly for a moment before his thin, almost colorless lips curled up to one side of his round face. He had an idea. "You know what, though? I think it's time we held a press conference to clear the air on these seditious allegations. Get something arranged for tomorrow."

So before long Addison had a major media event scheduled for the following afternoon. Coulter's advisors worked on the speech through the night and while the County Clerk put the finishing touches on his statement, Tom Sanders placed a call to John Gardner.

"Hello, professor," Gardner answered picking up the connection with an irritating cheerfulness dripping with insincerity.

"Hello, Mr. Gardner. If you have a few moments I'd like to talk to you about Meador Farms," Tom stated wasting little time at getting to his objective.

"Go ahead."

"I'd like to accept your offer."

"Refresh my memory. What offer was that?" Gardner asked in a patronizing tone.

The real estate mogul had a busy schedule and was sure to have multiple deals in the work at all times, Tom considered, but he couldn't have forgotten our conservation already. Nonetheless, Sanders summarized the counteroffer Gardner had made the previous week. "You'll exchange the Meador Farms property for our Prairie Parkway parcel plus two point five million dollars."

"Oh. Um, that could be a problem. I've started making some plans."

"I thought you made me an offer?" Tom replied trying hard not to sound overly indignant.

"We discussed a possible price, professor. When I didn't hear from you I figured that you weren't interested."

"I told you that I'd be back in touch with you within a week. It's only been six days since we met in your office so your offer should still stand."

"There's a lot of potential in the Meador Farms property. I'm pretty sure I want to hold onto it now."

Sanders seethed on his end of the connection. What was Gardner up to? Was he playing games, looking for more money? I'm not sure how much further the membership will let me go, the professor thought. But I've got to try.

"You said you're pretty sure you want to hold onto it. What does pretty sure mean, Mr. Gardner?"

"I suppose everything has its price. But, at this point, two and a half mill of extra cash just isn't that price."

Sanders knew he was walking into Gardner's negotiating trap. Nevertheless, he had to ask, "So what is the price?"

"Double what I said."

Sanders gulped. "That sounds a little extreme."

"I understand. You people probably don't have that kind of money."

Sanders lowered the communication device that he held in his hand, staring at it, pondering. He was ready to disconnect. Talking to Gardner any further seemed to be a waste of time because the man's words meant nothing. But then he suddenly had an idea; perhaps recognizing Gardner's lack of integrity was the key to dealing with him. Until an agreement is executed in verifiable form, whatever I say really doesn't mean a thing, Sanders rationalized. I can just string this along and wait for a more opportune moment. Then Tom said, "I think we can come up with the money you want."

"Really?"

"Yeah."

Gardner was caught off guard by the professor's persistence. "Okay," he responded. "But we'll have to hash out the details later because, as I'm sure you know, our County Clerk is about to start his press conference. There's no doubt he has something interesting to say."

"Of course. Now, you are negotiating in good faith this time, Mr. Gardner?"

"I'll call you back tomorrow," Gardner said, choosing not to acknowledge Sanders' obvious insinuation.

Tom immediately switched on his screen as he disconnected. "Maybe I shouldn't have added that last comment," he mumbled to himself before turning his attention to Coulter's prepared statement.

The County Clerk's image flashed across the screen. He stood behind a podium that hid the box he was perched atop. Coulter was always trying to mask his short stature, which he considered his only weakness.

"Residents of Ogle County," his voice boomed. "I am here today to ask for your continued support and to rebut false testimony recently submitted to certain media sources who irresponsibly reported such statements without checking their facts. First of all, the allegation that I illegally influenced the change in the federal land status of this great county is interesting to say the least. I am your faithful local servant; however, I have no jurisdiction over such federal matters."

Sanders chuckled as he listened to Coulter's statement. "Faithful servant? Did you mean to say self-serving demigod?"

Coulter continued, "As is often the case with such scurrilous assertions, there is one shred of truth in the story. I admit that I lobbied long and loud for the Mixed-Use designation so that we could fulfill our potential of becoming an important residential community and thriving commercial center. To create jobs and to provide suitable housing for the citizens of this county, I commissioned a report to demonstrate why Ogle's status should be changed. This was known as the Ogle Land Use Report. But, let me tell you, I did not write one sentence that appeared in that report. If there were any doctored facts included in the Ogle Land Use Report, then the responsible parties need be held accountable."

Sanders shook his head in wonderment. "Isn't hiring someone for the purpose of falsifying facts in a government report as much or more of a crime than writing the words for your self?" he muttered.

"The second allegation," Coulter went on, "maintains that I had property re-zoned for the favor of certain developers. This is another ridiculous claim. Show me the evidence. Unlike my accuser, what would I have to gain from such actions?"

By now it was pretty much public knowledge that Arthur Flemming was Coulter's accuser. But Coulter considered it beneath himself to acknowledge the traitorous developer by name. "To me, this whole thing tastes of sour grapes," he pitched to his audience. "This is a case of a disgruntled developer lashing out at me because his company has been unable to compete in our county where business and government are operated fairly and above board."

The seasoned politician gazed steadily into the camera and paused for effect after he had completed his prepared statement. Then he said, "Now, I'll take up to three questions from the media regarding these fictitious accusations and the unnecessarily costly federal probe that may result. After that, we'll move on to more important matters because I, for one, refuse to waste any more time with this man's slander. I trust that the citizens of Ogle County feel the same way."

# Chapter 38

Nathan Coulter's press conference failed to have the effect that he had hoped. Excluding his most ardent supporters, the public saw right through his tactics. They were vintage Coulter: bully his dissenters, including the media, and only play the game under his conditions. Some in his administration were worried but the County Clerk remained undaunted. "This news story will lose steam," he snarled hideously, " and after the election there are certain people who will pay."

Samuel Anthony recognized the facts. The Rural Reformers were coming from too far behind and the majority of the public didn't understand their platform. The party name in itself suggested that their agenda was too narrow to effectively govern over diverse county issues. Early on, Anthony and his advisors mulled over the idea of changing the party name but it was his sister who swayed them back. "They'd think we were selling out," Carrie warned. Now, with time running out, the party's only real hope at winning was through exposure and a demonstration that their policies were clearly superior to those of the current regime. But this could only be achieved by means of public debate and Coulter had wisely refused to be engaged.

After watching Coulter's attempt at hoodwinking the citizenry, Anthony considered one last approach. I'll hold my own press conference, he decided. Carrie liked the idea. "By appearing right on the heels of Coulter's speech you'll have the opportunity to present your contrasting style and beliefs. People might find you to be a refreshing alternative after listening to the crap they were being fed yesterday. In a way you'll be debating Coulter absent the formality of sharing the same stage."

So the day before the election Samuel Anthony held his news conference. Anthony hoped to reveal the depth of his abilities and persuade the public that the Rural Reformers were more than a radical fringe party. He made solid points on education, public safety and budget control. He sounded nothing like an uninformed candidate and he delivered his message with charisma. Anthony purposely limited the amount of time he devoted to speaking about the topic for which the Rural Reformers were known best. However, what he did say regarding land use reform was meaningful and forceful.

"As for the careless, unrelenting destruction of land in this county," he began on the topic, "they say you can't stop progress. But that line has gone stale. I say we can't progress until we challenge ourselves to define what progress really means. To make real progress we need cooperation and foresight.

'What developers and many others label as progress should be more aptly referred to as the leapfrog phenomenon. As an older community's infrastructure wears, those who are able move away, past newer settlements, to where land is cheap and to where they can find residence in the newest of the new developments. This perpetuates further decay in the communities they left behind. You can't fault individuals for seeking better opportunities but what this trend shows is that we need improved inter-governmental planning and cooperation. Let's all fix what's breaking and leave the promise of open space and a healthy earth to the children of our children."

The number of people who tuned in to hear Anthony's presentation was small compared to Coulter's audience. However, those who listened to him had to be impressed. After three terms of living under Coulter's rule the county needed new leadership. Tom Sanders had tuned in and could only hope that others who'd listened would be motivated enough to stand up and mandate the necessary change.

When Samuel Anthony was finished speaking Sanders felt encouraged to call John Gardner once more. "Are you ready to complete our trade yet?" Tom asked.

"Why, have you come up with the extra cash?"

"No, but I will."

"You better hurry because I'm thinking about sending more surveyors out to the site soon. I can't wait on you forever you know."

# Chapter 39

On Tuesday, April 6th Tom Sanders finished lecturing at three in the afternoon and hurriedly rushed across campus. The professor located his vehicle and pushed onward hoping to escape his melancholy as he drove toward Ogle County to cast his ballot. Samuel Anthony's uplifting speech and earnest campaign promises provided a temporary tonic but Tom's worries had soon returned. The stark reality saw Nathan Coulter on the verge of being elected to another term and John Gardner's amended asking price throwing the membership into an uproar. After intense weekend lobbying in front of the LPS, Sanders felt drained. His reservoir of courage and eloquence, a powerful combination melded in one and only recently manifested to lead his associates forward, now seemed tapped. His opportunity to save Meador Farms was evaporating.

As Tom left the polling place he called his wife. "Honey, I won't be home until later."

"Where are you, dear?"

"I just voted and now I'm heading out to Meador Farms in search of inspiration."

"But don't you want to follow the election returns from home this evening?" Marina asked forlornly.

"I can catch up on what's happened later. There's nothing we can do about it now anyway."

Tom switched his communication device to "off" when their conversation was finished and continued driving. He didn't mean to upset Marina but he couldn't go home. He just didn't see how he'd make good company. He was tired from thinking about land deals and about holding the LPS together. He was tired from thinking about elections and corrupt politicians. All he wanted to do at that moment was drive into the countryside unbothered, pretending to be a simple man leading a simple life.

After he crossed the river he began to focus on his sensation that the two-lane highway was establishing harmony with the surrounding landscape, narrowing ever so slightly in continuum as each mile passed. And when the road gradually rose out of the valley he opened his windows a quarter of the way down so that he could gulp in the cool spring air. The wind mussed his hair and tussled at the Meador site plan that he'd laid by his side. Other scraps of information blew from the passenger seat but he didn't care. Simple men had no concern for such details.

When Sanders came upon the property he slowed but did not stop. A sudden curiosity to see the village he and Tamara had spied from atop the ridgeline had come upon him. Simple men had time for diversions he reckoned as the road beyond Meador Farms led him on a curvy route that swept around neighboring farmsteads before reaching the church that established the gateway to one side of the village. The small town he entered consisted of no more than seventy-five modest but well manicured homes, a fuel station, grocery store and two small restaurants. Tom smiled when he noticed several villagers had large green posters trimmed in white lettering planted on their front lawns proclaiming, "Elect Rural Reform." "Now this is a community," he had barely finished whispering before he'd already reached the second church marking the other end of town. This was his cue to pull over and turn around.

On his way back through town an unassuming "Open" sign in the window of one of the cafes beckoned him to stop. Why not, he thought as he rolled into the empty lot. From there, he surveyed the one-story frame building that advertised nothing more than "Restaurant", mumbled "Looks good" and decided to go inside.

The waitress eyed Sanders cautiously when he came through the door. "You don't look like a trucker," she commented as Tom slid up to the counter and ordered a cup of coffee. The man was well dressed unlike most of her customers and usually, if they weren't truckers, her "passer-throughs" sat at a table and kept to themselves.

"No, Ma'am, I'm not."

"What brings you here then?" she asked indifferently.

"Seems like a nice place."

"It is."

"Say, have you heard how the election is going?"

"No, usually I don't follow that kind of stuff. I did vote this time, though," she added proudly.

"Well, good for you," Tom told her encouragingly.

The waitress was warming up to the stranger sensing that he was less pretentious than she had initially concluded. She topped off his coffee and continued, "I voted for that Samuel Anthony fellow. Happened to hear him talk on the news yesterday. What he said sounded right. Besides, I'm tired of Nathan Coulter. He seems mean."

The professor pursed his lips and shook his head up and down slowly. "I think you made an excellent choice."

Sanders could see through the window that the sun was creeping lower to the horizon so he swigged the rest of his coffee and settled his tab. He wanted to get back to Meador Farms before dark.

"See you around," the waitress called as he headed out the door.

Within five minutes Tom was back at the property's entrance. The driveway had been graded and widened. Not the prettiest sight but this won't disturb things too much he rationalized. We might have need for a small parking lot anyway. The public should be allowed access to come meander around here if they'd like.

"Listen to me," he said aloud to himself. "I'm talking as if we've already pulled off the trade." But he was feeling better, more confident that he would convince the society to muster whatever resources necessary to acquire the property. The journey out to the region including his saunter into the village had a more profound inspirational effect than he'd expected.

Tom parked and got out in front of the old Meador home that now had a large wooden placard slapped onto the facing next to the front door reading, "Gardner Development Company." He shook his head as he strolled past the sign and went around the back of the house to find the lane that followed along the pastures. His plan was to hike up to the ridgeline where he and Tamara had explored and watch the sunset from there.

A pair of cardinals flitted off the rail fencing attracting his attention as he turned the corner. Following their flight down the lane he noticed that a large section of fence had been removed from beyond where the birds had been perched. His gaze wandered toward the adjacent pasture where, well into the former grazing lands, Tom was stunned to see earth-moving machines lined neatly, ten in a row. Worse, the equipment had already devoured several acres of land and two massive piles of soil had been unceremoniously heaped to the side.

The sight was horrifying. Was this the wealthy man's progress to which Samuel Anthony had spoke? Surely John Gardner wasn't breaking ground here because he couldn't find anywhere else to establish affordable housing for the needy. "Our society has been victimized by our own success," Anthony had said. "Our basic needs are satiated and our more frivolous desires are at our fingertips. No more widgets need be invented. We rarely cultivate our fields to plant crops anymore. Our families are fed from the harvests of bio-engineered fields carved from rain forests that have been cleared the worldwide. Alas, our soil is tilled only to plant houses and palaces that feed the rich man's hobby."

Tears welled in the eyes of the President of the Land Preservation Society and esteemed professor of agricultural history as he looked out upon the orange sky dropping over the serene rolling hills that stood as a paradoxical backdrop to the scarred landscape. Sanders almost sensed Gardner's presence rushing past him in the lane to begin construction to spite the LPS, to spite Arthur Flemming and, ironically, even Nathan Coulter. Perhaps this was Gardner's way of getting back at them for being out-maneuvered at the auction and for being ignored by the County Clerk. Once the development mogul found out that Sanders really wanted to save Meador Farms he probably let go of any inclination to make a trade even if it meant forsaking a property more fitting with his portfolio.

Sanders stood for several minutes staring at the barren strip of pasture as if in mourning until suddenly he heard the hum of an engine followed by the thud of a door slamming around to the front side of the house. Someone had just arrived and was in a hurry. Tom tilted his head toward the old Meador residence expecting to see a man or possibly several men come racing around the side of the house. Technically he was trespassing but he was unafraid, not caring whether Gardner's men had come to accost him. Instead, he felt as how the last soldier might feel while standing in the face of the enemy. After seeing his comrades go down before him all fear was erased because there seemed nothing left to lose.

Sanders had anticipated correctly and someone did appear from around one corner of the structure; however, the figure was that of a woman. She dashed down the same lane that he had followed and was on a course that led straight toward him. As she neared her silhouette became clearer in the growing dusk and he began to recognize who it was.

"Tom!" she called out when she saw the professor's shadowy image off to the side of the lane leaning up against the pasture rail.

Sanders watched as Tamara continued running but he said nothing in response until she reached his side. "How did you know I was here?"

"Marina told me you were heading out here. She's very concerned but said you wanted to be left alone. But I don't care because you've gotta hear this. I've been trying to get hold of you. Why wouldn't you pick up?"

"I turned everything off. I've been trying to think of what to do next." Tom answered almost robotically.

Tamara's gaze finally reached past Tom to where the earth moving equipment was stationed in the field. "Oh my God!" she murmured. "They've already started."

She looked back at Tom her spirits doused even further by the sullen expression that enveloped his entire countenance. He had nothing to say. "So you haven't heard the news?" she asked.

"No."

"Coulter is out. Samuel Anthony was elected County Clerk. It's a miracle, Tom."

"That's great," Tom responded. But his demeanor portrayed his true emotions, which were incongruent with the words he spoke. He had dreamed of the day when the evil regime would be toppled and when the destruction would stop. But now with Coulter miraculously defeated devastation still lay before him.

Tom tried to gather himself by remembering what his father would tell him when he was a boy after he had lost a game or was feeling sad. Knowing that his son had a bright future in front of him he'd say, "Grieve no more and take solace in the good fortune that lies ahead."

When he was young he only pretended to understand what those words meant and at this moment comprehending their meaning was hardly less difficult. However, Tom knew that if his father could be with him now he'd be placing his arm around his shoulder professing that same belief.

Then more recent memories began streaming back. His wife and daughter had been attacked and he had come within inches of losing his life. The LPS had been placed at odds with one another and their first leader, who through his simple approach had enriched the professor's passion for the cause, had been murdered. But the kingpin behind these atrocities was finally vanquished. Was this the solace? Was this the good fortune for which he had been searching? The concept was almost unimaginable with topsoil swirling in the wind above his head but "Perhaps," Tom said turning toward Tamara, "It's not too late for us to begin celebrating the promise for reform."

His words sounded wise like they so often did to her but Tamara was concentrating on his eyes trying to read them. They were vulnerable, gentler than she'd ever noticed. She could tell that they were asking a question more so than imparting wisdom. She felt a yearning to embrace him and to provide him with answers. "You're right," she said instead. "Perhaps we should be celebrating."

So they left Meador Farms and the lands beyond the river uncertain of ever recapturing images of open spaces how once etched in their consciousness. But when they crossed the bridge Tom called his wife hoping that she might start chilling the champagne.